Zero at the b

'The police,' said Susan Lyne, 'seem to be taking an interest in your undesirable neighbours.'

'Quite time too.'

Fiona Laslett joined her sister at the bedroom window. For a moment or two they both watched the policeman in the road talking to the man from the cottage at the corner.

But the police weren't interested in their neighbours – at least not yet. Later they would return in numbers, to investigate the inescapable fact of violent death. But at present they were only inquiring, rather quietly and casually, about a domestic python that had strayed from nearby Bright's Farm, where a number of rare animals, including an eagle owl, a goshawk and a peregrine falcon were among the household satellites.

Elizabeth Ferrar's novel, first published in 1967, has pace and excitement, the characters are studied and true, and the background is colourful. The training of a falcon is described in some detail. But the story is also a classical puzzle with an extraordinarily ingenious mystery. The reader is fooled by a very simple trick, and will look back with admiration at the clue which disguises the final revelation.

Books by Elizabeth Ferrars

ZERO AT THE BONE

Elizabeth Ferrars

Constable · London

First published in Great Britain 1967
by William Collins Sons & Co Ltd
Copyright © 1967 by M. D. Brown
The right of Elizabeth Ferrars to be
identified as the author of this work
has been asserted by her in accordance
with the Copyright, Designs and
Patents Act 1988
Reprinted 1996
by Constable & Company Ltd
3 The Lanchesters, 162 Fulham Palace Road
London W6 9ER
ISBN 0 09 476070 5
Printed and bound in Great Britain by
Hartnolls Ltd, Bodmin

A CIP catalogue record for this book
is available from the British Library

Several of nature's people
I know and they know me;
I feel for them a transport
Of cordiality;

But never met this fellow,
Attended or alone,
Without a tighter breathing,
And zero at the bone.

Emily Dickinson

1

'The police,' said Susan Lyne, 'seem to be taking an interest in your undesirable neighbours.'

'Quite time too.'

Fiona Laslett joined her sister at the bedroom window. For a minute or two they watched the policeman in the road talking to the man from the cottage at the corner.

The cottage was an unattractive brick box which had been built about fifty years before to house the family of one of the labourers at the nearby farm, or what had then been a farm. Most of its land had been sold off long ago and the couple who lived in the old farmhouse now made their living, not by farming, but by writing very successful books for children.

The man from the cottage was packing suitcases into the boot of his pale blue Anglia while the girl who no one would believe was his wife hung over the garden gate, doubled up with laughter. The breeze blew her yellow hair in all directions and puffed out the skirt of her cotton dress like a parachute.

The two men appeared to be talking gravely, then the constable turned to the girl and said something to her which she answered by giving her head an exaggerated shake from side to side, which set her yellow hair swinging. She spun on her heel and darted back into the cottage. The man shrugged his shoulders, slammed down the lid of the boot, locked it and got into the car. As he drove off the constable started to push his bicycle towards the Lasletts' gate.

Their house, like the cottage, had been built on a piece of land that had once belonged to the farm, but was only two years old, had been designed more or less by Fiona herself, and was comfortable, labour-saving and set charmingly among trees. Fiona loved it with only a little less fervour than she loved her husband, Arthur Laslett.

'He's coming here,' she said, watching the policeman. 'He's probably selling tickets for something.'

She turned to leave the bedroom. She was a slender woman, twenty-eight years old, smoothly brown and glowing with health, with a gentle, dreamy face and red-gold hair.

Susan stayed at the window and saw the door of the cottage re-open and the girl come out and stand looking after the policeman. Suddenly she started laughing again and ran back indoors. Through a window Susan could see her moving about in the small front room.

'D'you know, I believe she's dancing!' Susan exclaimed. For the girl had spread her arms out and was whirling round and round. 'She looks an absolute child. Much too young to be married.'

She herself was only twenty-one, but she felt that a gulf of unnumbered years divided her from the laughing, spinning girl.

'That's what a lot of people think,' Fiona said. 'They wouldn't serve her at the pub when the two of them first arrived, but their story is that she's nineteen.'

Susan began to say that that wasn't possible, but the policeman, who had turned in at the Lasletts' gate, had just rung the doorbell and Fiona went running downstairs to open the door while Susan returned to her unpacking.

She had only just arrived from London and her skin still had a London pallor, but in other ways she looked very like Fiona, and not so very much the younger. There was already a faint tracing of frown-lines on her forehead and her gaze was wary and grave. She had thinner features than Fiona's, moodier and less perfect, and she wore the kind of clothes in which Fiona wouldn't have been seen dead. Today she was wearing, and had travelled down from London in, black jeans, a flapping shirt of emerald green and straw sandals.

Tumbling out of her suitcase the shoes and the books that were all that was left in it, Susan shut it and put it away at the bottom of the dress-cupboard, kicked the shoes under the bed and

6

gathered up the books she had brought, intending to work hard through the long vacation, and began to arrange them on an empty shelf. There was a formidable row of them. She was working for a degree in zoology at London University and next year was her final year and life was becoming serious.

However, before she had finished arranging the books, Fiona called to her to come downstairs and Susan let them fall in a heap on the table. There they would probably remain for the next three months. Fiona, at any rate, wouldn't touch them. She had learnt that there was something incomprehensibly sacred about the disorder in which Susan's books, notebooks and miscellaneous scribblings were generally to be found.

Going downstairs, Susan joined Fiona and the policeman at the open front door. Like the girl from the cottage, both of them were laughing.

'Yes, just as you say, Mrs Laslett,' the constable was saying. 'Looked at like that, I know it's sort of comical. But then again, it isn't exactly a joke. I mean, you could have a bad scare if you weren't prepared, so that's why I'm going around warning people to look out.'

'Oh, of course, and I'm very grateful to you for coming,' Fiona said. She introduced Susan, 'This is my sister, Miss Lyne. Susan, Mr Burke is looking for a python.'

'A *python*?' Susan said. 'Is that a make of car?' She was thinking of cars with such names as Jaguar and Hawk. 'Has it been stolen?'

'No, a python, a snake, an enormous snake,' Fiona said, 'that coils itself around you and crushes your bones to pulp and swallows you down whole.'

'They don't really, you know,' Susan said. 'That's been vastly exaggerated.' She looked at the constable. 'You don't mean a live python, do you?'

'Yes, Miss Lyne, I do, it's very much alive and kicking, so to speak, as far as we know,' he answered. 'But you needn't be afraid it'll harm you in any way, or so I understand. It's only ten foot long and Mr Riscoe says it's not likely to be dangerous if you don't scare it. I'm just spreading the word around about it being lost in case anyone sees it unexpectedly and becomes unnecessarily alarmed.'

'I wonder how one avoids scaring a ten foot python,' Susan said. 'Ought one to stand still and talk to it soothingly or what?'

Fiona laughed again. 'Isn't it just like Rob Riscoe to say a thing like that? I hope I'm not the person who finds it.'

Robert Riscoe and his wife Nina were the couple who lived in the old farmhouse and wrote children's books. They were the Lasletts' closest friends in the village.

'If you do find the snake, Mrs Laslett,' the policeman said, 'I'm sure the best thing would be just to leave it alone and notify the police or else Mr Riscoe himself. But I don't fancy it'll come as far as this. More likely it'll stay somewhere in the woods. Not that I know anything much about a snake's habits. I'm just going by Mr Riscoe. He says it's a friendly reptile and won't be hungry for some time because it had just had a good meal when it escaped.'

'I wonder how long it'll take to get hungry again and what it'll do if you don't find it before it does,' Fiona said. 'How long ago did they lose it?'

'Three days, Mr Riscoe said. But I'm sure we'll find it soon. Seems it's a new acquisition, answers to the name of Adam. I mean, that's what they call it. Sounds kind of queer to me. Adam wasn't a snake, he was the one who had all that trouble with one, eh? It was Mrs Riscoe let it get away, seemingly. She didn't fasten the cage properly after feeding it and the minute she turned her back it was gone. They feed it on rats, she said. White rats.' A sudden shudder ran through Mr Burke's muscular frame. 'I don't mind admitting, I'm like you, Mrs Laslett, I hope I'm not the one who finds it. There's something about snakes. If ever I dream about them I wake up screaming.'

He grinned, wished them good-evening and retreated to the bicycle that he had left at the gate.

Shutting the door, Fiona turned towards the sitting-room.

'I wouldn't put it past Nina to have left the cage open on purpose,' she said. 'I sometimes think she doesn't love the live-stock nearly as much as Rob imagines. Which reminds me, Susan, I've a message for you from Nina. She wants to know if you'd like your old job back for the summer.'

A year ago, when Susan had spent most of the summer here, she had done some secretarial work for the Riscoes.

Strolling across the room to the open french window, she sat down on the doorstep. The room was long and low, with plain white walls, a polished teak floor and slim-legged Scandinavian furniture with black upholstery and plenty of small gay cushions. Sunshine flooded in through the open window.

Frowning slightly, Susan looked out across the lawn and the rosebeds into the cool shadow of the woods that surrounded the garden. Through the tree-tops she could see the twisted chimneys of the Riscoes' house. The breeze had dropped. The late afternoon was warm and very quiet. A haziness faintly masked the blue of the sky. A thrush's song from deep in the wood sounded as clear and as close as if the bird were singing in the garden.

Fiona poured out two gin-and-tonics.

'You've gone very quiet all of a sudden,' she said as she brought a drink to Susan. 'You aren't worrying about that snake, are you?'

'Not the snake.'

'What's on your mind then?'

'Nothing special.'

'Something to do with the Riscoes?' Fiona sat down on the long black sofa. In a crisp white cotton dress she looked very graceful and cool. 'I thought you liked them.'

'I do.'

'D'you know, last year I thought you were half in love with Rob. But perhaps it was just with his zoo. I know you were crazy about that hawk of his. We hardly saw anything of you all the time you were here.'

After a little pause Susan replied, 'It just happens this year that I've lots of work of my own I ought to be doing.'

'Well, if you don't want the job, you've only to say so. They won't hold it against you.'

'You didn't promise them anything?'

'Of course not. I only said I'd give you their message and that you'd probably be along to see them tomorrow morning to talk it over.'

'Then they'll talk me into it.'

'That'll be the day. I've never been able to talk you into doing anything you didn't want to do.'

9

Susan looked round at Fiona, smiling. 'That's what you think. You just didn't notice the times I gave in.'

'Oh well then, ring them up and put them off,' Fiona said placidly. 'Or I'll do it, if you like. I didn't mean to get you involved in anything. It's just that I mentioned to Nina that you were coming and she started begging me at once to get you to take the job on again. Their most recent secretary got married a week or two ago and went off to live in Manchester and they can't find a satisfactory replacement. Nina's reduced to typing out their latest book with her own two fingers.'

'I'll go over and see them, anyway,' Susan said. 'D'you know if they're alone, or are they flooded with visitors? Last year they were always flooded with visitors. The atmosphere got perfectly hysterical.'

'But you loved it last year,' Fiona said, 'I know you did.'

'Yes . . . But this year I've really got to do some solid work or I'll make a fool of myself when the exams come round. I've got to get at least a good second or I shan't get a research grant.'

'So you've made up your mind that's what you want to do – research?'

Fiona looked dubious, as if she thought this overambitious in any sister of hers. She herself had taken a diploma in domestic science, which she had later declared had been a complete waste of time and money, since she had learnt far more in six months of managing her own home than in the two years that she had spent at the college. And she could have enjoyed herself so much more during those two years if she hadn't spent them listening to dull lectures, taking notes that she would never look at again and reading stupid books.

But Fiona, until her marriage, had always been the wild one of the family. Susan's passion for acquiring more and more education was something that she had never been able to understand, unless it was their father's nature coming out in her. He had been rector in a country parish in Suffolk and as singularly incompetent at dealing with the problems of his parishioners as with those of his two good-looking daughters. But he had loved books, nearly all books, and also paper and ink as devotedly as Susan was beginning to show signs of loving them. If he had lived, Fiona thought, Susan in the end would no doubt have supplanted her as his favourite daughter, would have lived with him, perhaps, taken care of him in his old age, run the parish for him. . . .

Fiona began to smile. That was going a bit far. You could trust Susan to have the whole place up against her in a month. She had no tact, no patience and not much understanding of other people. And a B.Sc., not to mention the Ph.D. that would probably follow, wasn't the best of training for settling down contentedly to church work in a country parish. Besides, with that red-gold hair, hanging heavy and straight to her shoulders, and that lovely figure she wasn't going to stay unmarried for long.

Yet Susan hadn't so far shown much interest in men. The only one in whom Fiona had noticed her showing any had been Rob Riscoe, and he was forty and married.

Not that that made it impossible. Only rather unfortunate.

Susan had turned away again to gaze absently across the sunlit garden at the Riscoes' house. She asked abruptly, 'Fiona, those people we saw just now from the cottage – you wrote how awful they were, but what's really the matter with them?'

'The Taylors? Why, everything,' Fiona said. 'They're just generally impossible.'

'Really impossible, or is that just your snobbishness coming out?'

'Both, and why not? Why shouldn't I be a snob with people who are disgustingly rude to me when I try to be friendly and who keep the place like a pigsty. And there's something very odd about them too. Arthur says the trouble is that the girl's obviously below the age of consent and must have run away from home and so they're in hiding.'

'Then they aren't friends of the Riscoes'?'

'Not that I know of.'

'But the cottage belongs to the Riscoes, doesn't it? Why did they let it to those people if they're really so awful?'

'They probably didn't bother to find out anything about them. You know how vague they are. After all, who else would simply lose a ten foot python? But why are you worrying about the Taylors? They don't bother us. When I wrote I was just feeling

11

disappointed that there weren't going to be nicer people living in the cottage, as they're our nearest neighbours.'

'I keep thinking about that girl laughing and dancing all by herself in there,' Susan said. 'It was crazy and yet in a way it was beautiful. It must be wonderful to be able to go mad like that. Anyway, it looks as if something I heard about them isn't true.'

'What did you hear?'

'Oh, nothing important.'

'It can't have been so unimportant or you wouldn't have mentioned it.'

'Really it was.'

'Well, whom did you hear it from, whatever it may have been?'

'Conrad Ives.'

Fiona's eyebrows shot up. 'Have you been seeing him?'

'Occasionally.'

'I didn't realise that. Where have you seen him?'

'In London, of course. You don't think I'd have come down here to see him without coming to see you too.'

'No – no, I suppose not, though you can be terribly secretive sometimes. And I didn't realise . . .' Fiona hesitated. It was very easy to put a foot wrong with Susan. And Conrad Ives, who was a reporter on a small and extremely insignificant local weekly, and who had managed to scrape acquaintance with her and Fiona at last year's village fête, of which, incidentally, he had written a ludicrously flowery and inaccurate account, did not strike Fiona as the right sort of person for Susan to be seeing much of.

'He's nice, isn't he?' she said cautiously.

Once, when she had been twenty, she had almost proposed marriage to a certain man of whom she had been seeing a good deal, because an officious friend had told her that he was not only penniless but unstable, promiscuous, and altogether dreadful. And he really had been unstable, exceedingly lecherous, and also without intelligence or enterprise, and now was working in a garage somewhere, making only a few hundred a year. And money, after all, was a very pleasant thing to have at your disposal. Fiona gave a contented glance at her gleaming teak floor and Swedish furniture and was just about to ask Susan how she liked the new abstract painting over the fireplace when she heard the slam of a car door. The slam of the car door was all that was ever heard of the Bentley when Arthur drove up in it. Jumping to her feet, Fiona ran to meet him.

Susan followed and was given an affectionate clap on the shoulder and a peck on the cheek by her brother-in-law when he had finished kissing his wife, an operation which was not over in a moment. Arthur Laslett, after a few years in the army, which had taken him to Egypt, Cyprus and some other trouble spots, had become a chartered accountant and now worked for a firm of scientific instrument makers whose main factory and administrative offices were in Swelsden, the town seven miles away, of which the so-called village in which he and Fiona lived was really an outlying suburb.

Arthur was forty, fair-haired, a little bald, short and stocky, with a square, ruddy, smiling face and light grey eyes, which were singularly alive and very friendly. He and Fiona had been married three years.

Pouring out a drink for him, Fiona told him about the escaped python.

'I'm ahead of you,' he said. 'I stopped in at the Dragon just now and the place was buzzing with the story.'

'You know, you're becoming an old drunk,' Fiona said. 'I believe you stop in at the Dragon every evening, and then want more drink when you get home.'

'Listen to her, Susan,' he said. 'Is that kind or wifely? She knows I only do it to be able to bring her home some gossip, which is life-blood to her. For instance, I can tell you this evening that your ten foot python is actually twelve foot long.'

'That's wrong, it's only ten,' Fiona said. 'That's what Jim Burke said, didn't he, Susan?'

'Ah, well, growth and decay are natural processes,' Arthur said. 'If a story doesn't grow it soon dies on you.'

He took his drink upstairs, to reappear presently in flannels and an open-necked shirt and to help himself to another drink and stretch out on the sofa.

But he was a man who could not sit still. In a moment, glass in hand, he went out into the garden and strolled about, looking

13

critically at his roses. His army training still showed in the way he held himself. His shoulders were very square, his back was very straight. Sometimes he tenderly handled a beautiful bloom, sometimes stooped swiftly to tear out a weed. Once he returned as far as the french window to say, ' "I had an aunt in Yucatan, who bought a python from a man. . . ." Belloc, isn't it? I don't remember exactly what happened to the aunt, but I know it was disagreeable. A lot of disagreeable things seem to happen to aunts in light verse, I don't know why. My own aunts were beautiful and charming women who married rich, adoring men who let them have their own way in everything. And now they're all showing signs of living into a healthy and riotous old age, so that Fiona and I will never inherit anything from them.'

'Your trouble, darling,' Fiona said, pausing before going out to the kitchen to put the finishing touches to dinner, 'is that you find all women beautiful and charming. You've still to learn discrimination.'

She said it with happy smugness. She had never had one moment's doubt that Arthur found her more beautiful and more charming than all the other women he good-naturedly admired.

Fiona was a very good cook. Her chilled cucumber soup was delicious. So were the lamb cutlets with tiny green peas from the garden. The strawberries, from the garden too, were perfect in their ripeness and freshness.

Afterwards, while she stayed to stack the dishes in the dishwasher, she sent Susan out to join Arthur in the garden. He had taken his secateurs out with him and was moving from flowerbed to flowerbed, snipping off any slightly fading bloom. From the kitchen window the humming sound of the dishwasher followed them through the twilight like the humming of a monstrous wasp. A haze of midges danced about their heads. It seemed even hotter, more airless than in the earlier evening.

Arthur's thoughts had returned to the python.

'Snakes aren't exactly my idea of congenial pets,' he remarked, slapping at his cheek where a midge was biting him. 'Still, everyone to his taste. The Riscoes are real characters, aren't they? I don't know where we'd be without them.'

Calling someone a character was Arthur's way of saying that, fond as he might be of this particular person, he would like him even better if his hobbies were bridge and golf instead of eccentric things like keeping pythons and other curious pets.

He went on, 'All the same, I wonder if it might be sensible to keep the downstairs windows shut till the thing's been caught – though I suppose it could slither up a drainpipe if it happened to think of it. What d'you think, Susan?'

She shook her head. 'I don't know.'

'Oh, I'm sure you do really. I'm sure you know all about that sort of thing.' He said it as if he felt that Susan were being unduly modest and needed to be reassured of her wide knowledge and intelligence.

'Really, I don't,' she said. She had never found it possible to convey to Arthur that a zoologist was not someone who worked in a zoo and who understood the rearing and taming of all animals from guinea-pigs to African elephants.

'Well, I suppose one shouldn't worry.' He lit a cigarette and blew smoke at the hovering midges to drive them away. 'If this were India and there was a whole nest of pythons in that wood one probably wouldn't give them a thought. Now tell me how things are with you, Susan. How's the work going? Still as interesting as ever?'

She changed the subject with determination. 'The Riscoes want me to do some typing for them again,' she said. 'I suppose I ought to do it, if they're in a jam.'

'But you're on holiday, aren't you?' Arthur said. 'I shouldn't do anything you don't really want to. They're always in a jam, anyway.'

'I think Fiona wants me to do it,' Susan said.

'Well, don't let her push you around. It's a little habit she has and it'll do her good not to get away with it for once. I'm no use to her there, I always give in.'

Susan knew that this was not true. She had always been aware of an obstinate strength in Arthur, behind his easygoing charm. Fiona would never get away with any more than he wanted. And probably, Susan thought, knowing how badly Fiona had needed someone to cling to when their father died, it had been that core of steel in Arthur that had attracted her to him.

15

It would not have attracted Susan. She respected it and had grown very fond of Arthur, but her own need was for something quite different. It was for someone far subtler than Arthur, more colourful, and positively more intelligent than she was herself, or she would soon grow bored with him, someone whom it would not be quite so easy to love and to understand . . .

She went up to bed early. Her room looked cool. It had pale grey walls, white curtains and a light green bedspread. There were some sweetly scented sprays of honeysuckle in a little vase on the table by the bed. Yet the air felt warmer than ever. The window was wide open, but not a breath stirred the curtains.

Going to the window, Susan leant out. The darkness was like a smothering curtain, hiding all but the faint outline of the bracken-covered hillside that sloped up from the road opposite to the window. To the left, where the village began, she could see a sprinkling of lights, but there were none in the other direction. The yellow-haired girl must have gone to bed even earlier than Susan had herself. The cottage at the corner was only a block of shadow, blending with the shadows of the trees growing near it. It looked a lonely and mysterious place.

While Susan stood there, her elbows on the window-sill, an owl hooted. She knew from the sound that it was a wild owl, going its predatory way about its normal affairs, and not Orlando, Rob Riscoe's tame owl, if tame was the right word for the monstrous creature, an eagle owl, which he had brought home from Norway, and with which he sometimes prowled out in the evening to let the bird fly at the end of a creance, that slender line which, in the early stage of training a bird, tethers the fierce, beautiful falcon to its master until it has learnt and can be trusted to return of itself to the glove.

Susan had never really taken to Orlando. If ever she had seen pure hatred in a pair of eyes, it seemed to her that it had been in those of the captive owl. But that, of course, like the notion that owls were wise because they happened to look rather as if they were wearing spectacles, was only regrettable anthropomorphism. Poor thing, Orlando was just a normal, uncomplicated bird, living according to the nature that God had given him, except that he had been unlucky enough to be caught. . . .

Susan slept soundly that night in spite of the heat. She woke late. Getting out of bed, yawning and stretching, she was just in time to see a furniture van go slowly down the road. It stopped at the cottage. The girl with the yellow hair was waiting for it at the gate. When two men climbed down from the van she took them into the cottage.

So, after all, what Conrad Ives had said about the Taylors was true. They were moving out. And if that much of what he had told her was true, probably the rest of it, the part of it that really mattered to Susan, was true too.

With her heart suddenly pounding, she began to dress hurriedly.

2

Susan put on the same black jeans as yesterday and the straw sandals, but a different shirt. This one was of big yellow and black checks. Running downstairs, she saw Arthur just driving off to Swelsden in the Bentley. Mrs Whicker, the daily help, who came for four hours every morning, was in the sitting-room, pushing the electric polisher dreamily backwards and forwards over the teak floor. Fiona, in shorts, a halter and a pair of gardening gloves, was in the garden, spraying weed-killer on to the short drive from the garage gate. Her bare back and her long, slim legs were as smoothly brown as her face and her arms. Her hair shone like burnished copper in the bright morning sunshine.

Susan went into the dining-room, swallowed a cup of coffee, slapped butter on to a piece of toast and ran out into the road, eating the toast as she ran. Fiona called something out to her, but Susan hurried on as if she had not heard. She went towards the cottage.

It was about fifty yards from the Lasletts' house, where the road divided into two narrow lanes. The left-hand lane wound across open country until it joined the main road from London to Swelsden. The right-hand lane, which went straight like an avenue between tall beeches, had a wooden signpost pointing along it, which said, 'To Bright's Farm only – No Thoroughfare'. The cottage stood on the triangle of ground between the two lanes.

At the moment the furniture van almost blocked the way to Bright's Farm, the Riscoes' home. Susan saw at once that there had been no need for her haste. While the two men carried a decrepit sofa from the cottage to the gate and heaved it up into the van, the girl with the yellow hair wandered idly about the garden, looking bored and listless, as if she did not know what to do with herself while the men were working. She was wearing a brief sleeveless black dress and great plastic ear-rings and was carrying a big white plastic handbag. She did not see Susan until they were almost face to face with one another across the fence, with only a few yards between them.

The girl started then, opening her eyes wide. They were dark eyes, not the right colour to go with her yellow hair, and her skin had the olive pallor of someone who was naturally dark. Her upper lip had a faint dark shadow of down along it. But at this short distance Susan could see that the hair had been bleached. It had been unevenly, amateurishly done. The girl's features looked soft and unformed, like her small, vigorous body.

'Hallo,' she said, after staring for a moment.

'Hallo,' said Susan.

'I thought you was Mrs Laslett, but you're not.'

'No.'

'You just look like her.'

'She's my sister,' Susan explained. 'I'm staying with her.'

'You didn't want me then?'

'Well . . . ' Susan hesitated. 'No, not specially.'

'You didn't come looking for me?'

'No, I was just passing.' Susan had a feeling that there was relief on the girl's face. 'I'm on my way to see the Riscoes.'

'You can tell them goodbye from me then,' the girl said with sudden gaiety. 'They'll be glad to see the back of us. And I'm not going to miss them either, you can tell them that too, if you like.' She laughed happily. But then she began to tug uneasily at her lower lip. 'No, better not, better not say anything. I got a way of wanting to say things I shouldn't. Where d'you come from? London?'

'That's where I'm living now,' Susan replied.

'How long are you here for?'

'A few weeks. Or perhaps not so long. It depends.'

'I'm going to London,' the girl said eagerly. 'Mr Taylor went on

19

there yesterday. He went to get the new place ready. I'm glad I'm going to London. It's what I always wanted.'

'Don't you like it here?' Susan asked.

'Oh, it's all right, I dare say, if you like gardening and that, but it's not what I bargained for when I started out. It's not what we done at first. We travelled around a lot, staying in hotels and eating in restaurants, and I got some nice clothes, some lovely clothes. I wish I could show you. . . .' She was talking faster and faster, the words spilling out as if they had been dammed up for a long time. 'But what can you do with nice clothes here? Hand them over to the moths? Say, "Take them and welcome!" I tell you, sometimes I looked at my things hanging up in the cupboard and I cried, I really did, I cried like a kid. Then I'd take them out and turn the hems up or something. Soft, wasn't it? Jack said it was soft. "Wait!" I said to him. "You wait till we're in London. You won't say I'm soft then. I'll get a job and some money for myself and I'll throw this whole lot out and buy some new things and then – then I'll . . ." ' She paused at last, an uncertain smile lingering on her full young lips.

'But you don't come from London, do you?' Susan said.

The question blotted all expression from the girl's face.

'I do,' she said. 'I do come from London. Where d'you think I come from?'

'I don't know – from somewhere in the Midlands, perhaps.'

'Well, I don't.' Her voice rose, as if by speaking louder she could make what she said more convincing. 'I come from London.' She turned on her heel.

As she walked away, Susan called after her, 'Just a minute! Do wait a minute! Do you know who's moving into this cottage after you?'

But the girl did not pause or answer and in a moment had vanished into the cottage.

Walking slowly, with the frown-lines on her forehead more marked than usual, Susan went on down the lane to Bright's Farm.

The house was still called that, although it was longer than anyone living could remember since any Bright had lived in it. It was about a quarter of a mile from the cottage. The woods reached almost to the house, which was a pleasant, rambling old building of mellowed brick with a steep roof pierced by the dormer windows of the attics, and twisted chimneys. A narrow belt of rather weedy lawns and a few untidy flowerbeds surrounded the house, but behind it was a large and flourishing vegetable garden, full of unusual things: sweetcorn, sweet peppers, courgettes, asparagus, artichokes. The Riscoes could never have been content to grow the same plants as other people any more than to keep the same domestic pets.

Nina Riscoe was on the look-out for Susan and came hurrying to the door to meet her before she had time to knock.

Nina was a thin, restless, talkative woman of thirty-five, with a nervous, vivid face and long, bony hands with which she stabbed at the air to add incomprehensible emphasis to what she was saying. She had short, shaggy brown hair and big, remarkably beautiful grey eyes. There was usually a vague peasant air about her clothes. She liked full, bright-coloured skirts and embroidered blouses. Today her skirt was scarlet and her blouse white muslin, embroidered in black. And as so often when Susan had seen her, she had Touchie, a small brown monkey, perched on her shoulder.

'Susan, this is angelic of you,' Nina cried as she grasped Susan's arm. She talked straight on as usual in swift staccato sentences. 'You haven't any idea what a help it's going to be. I've been going absolutely distracted since Gladys left us. Everything's been getting out of hand. The house, the garden, everything. I'm such a fool with a typewriter, it takes me hours longer to type a thing out than to write it in the first place.'

The room into which she took Susan was low, with beams in the ceiling and an uneven stone floor. The furniture consisted of a large kitchen table with a mess of papers and a typewriter on it, an old Windsor chair and some bookshelves on which reference books stood cheek by jowl with jars of home-made jams and pickles.

'Rob's out at the moment,' Nina hurried on, 'but I expect he'll be back soon. You heard about Adam getting loose, I expect. The python. Rob's out searching for him again, although he called the police in about it yesterday. He insisted on doing that in case

21

someone suddenly saw Adam and killed him, poor thing. Rob doesn't worry much about the person who sees him. He blames me, of course, for letting Adam get away, and I suppose it really was my fault. Yet I only turned my back for a moment, Susan, honestly I did, just a moment. And I ask you, how can I do everything? This typing, I mean – I'd been up half the night trying to get it done. The manuscript's all there, and Rob's finished the illustrations, and as usual we want the money, because we want to go abroad next month. So you see, I felt I'd simply got to get the thing off . . . When I heard you were coming back I was wild with delight – wild, I tell you. And I think it's sweet of you, Susan, I do truly, to give up the time to us when there must be masses of other things you'd sooner do.'

Susan smiled. It was not really at Nina but at Touchie, who was half-sheltering behind Nina's head but kept peeping out shyly at Susan. She put out a hand to stroke him. With a chattering cry he leapt out of reach on to the top of a bookcase.

'Silly thing,' Nina said. 'He's always irritating when we have visitors here, just like a child who's afraid he won't be given enough attention. It's lucky you aren't wearing any jewellery. He'd probably try to snatch it. He adores anything that glitters. Touchie, you damned nuisance, come down, will you?'

It took more coaxing than that to bring him down, but at last he came. Susan had sat down at the table and taken the cover off the typewriter.

'What do you and Rob do about the animals when you go abroad?' she asked. 'They're such an odd mixture for anyone else to take on.'

'Usually only one of us goes and the other stays to look after things,' Nina said. 'It's more of a tie than children, because you can take children with you, or hand them over to a grandmother who's delighted to have them, or thinks she will be till she's actually had to put up with them day in, day out, for a little while. I remember my own grandmother used to welcome me with tears of joy and shoo me out after a week or two with smiles of unbounded delight. Actually, Rob and I haven't been away together for years and years. But this year, with Jocelyn and Annette coming to the cottage . . . ' She pulled herself up.

Making one of her curious gestures, which was as if she were brushing something away from her, she turned her back on Susan and began to fiddle with some flowers in a bowl on the window-sill. 'There I go, talking too much, as usual. What I just said is supposed to be confidential. But you remember Jocelyn, don't you, Susan? Rob's brother. He was staying with us last year when you were working for us.'

Susan rolled some sheets of paper and carbon into the type-writer. Her fingers suddenly felt cold and clumsy.

'Yes, of course,' she said, staring hard at the paper, staring through it and far away. 'Of course I remember him.'

'Poor Jocelyn,' Nina went on, 'he was in an awful state all that summer. Annette was giving him hell. And you were the only person who could cheer him up, going all those long walks with him.'

'It's true then,' Susan said quietly. 'He's married.'

'Yes, but how did you hear? As I said, it's supposed to be frightfully confidential.'

'I heard it from Conrad Ives. He told me Jocelyn had got married and given up his teaching job and was coming to live here in your cottage while he got on with writing his next play.'

'Yes, well, it's all perfectly true.' Nina sounded flustered and defensive. Susan began to wonder if it had been from her, in one of her too expansive moods, that Conrad had heard the story. 'He's only paying us a nominal rent for the cottage, but he's going to look after the animals for us when we go away. And for some reason, it all had to be secret. Personally I hate these hush-hush things. For one thing, they always get out, then you feel such a fool when you've been doing your best not to talk, and suddenly realise that everyone else knows all there is to know already. Besides, there's an awful self-importance about that kind of secrecy. Don't you think so? Jocelyn may be a success at the moment, but do you honestly believe anyone is so interested in him that they'd be a nuisance here to him and Annette if they want to be left alone? After all, who ever remembers a new dramatist's name? It's less important to most people than the name of the wig-maker. They only really remember the names of the stars. Now if he'd married one of them it would be

23

different, but Annette's a mere schoolmistress, beautiful as she is. I've never liked her much, but I do admit she's beautiful. Did you ever go to see the play, Susan? Don't ever tell Jocelyn I said so, but I thought it was lousy.'

'I thought it was pretty good.' Susan's voice was subdued and the blank sheet of paper in the typewriter still seemed to be absorbing most of her attention. 'Awfully good. Marvellous, really.'

Nina shook her head. 'All that analytical stuff about those brothers who hated each other, it bored me to tears. It was all so horribly cerebral. People simply aren't like that. It's odd when you think what a warm sort of person Jocelyn is that he can't put any warmth or life into his characters. And the murder at the end isn't the kind I like. All that horrible red blood that got on to everything – it made me feel sick.'

'Blood *is* rather red,' Susan observed.

'Yes, and in its proper place I can stand the sight of it as well as most people. You'd know that if you'd seen me butchering rats to keep Orlando fed on good fresh meat. But when I go out for what I think is going to be a nice evening . . . Ugh!'

'Jocelyn told me he never meant to have all that blood slopping about,' Susan said. 'It was the producer's idea and they had quite a fight about it.'

'And of course, Jocelyn gave in. He always gives in. You'd think he actually enjoys being a doormat for everyone to wipe their feet on.'

Susan shrugged her shoulders. 'He told me he gave in because he'd have been a fool to get across everyone when he was only just getting started doing the thing he wanted to do more than anything else on earth.'

Nina turned away from the window to look at Susan curiously. 'You must have seen him recently.'

'About a month ago, I think it was.' Susan said it as casually as if she had not in fact been able to count the number of days, almost the number of hours, since she had last seen Jocelyn Riscoe. 'He took me to see the play.'

'And he didn't tell you he was getting married.'

'No.'

24

'He may not have known it himself a month ago,' Nina said thoughtfully. 'He didn't tell us anything either until it was done.'

'When is he – when are they moving in?' Susan asked.

'On Saturday. Jocelyn is, anyway. I believe Annette's taking some gang of schoolgirls to Rome or somewhere. She isn't giving up her job yet. They're very prudent people, both of them. Annette isn't going to stop teaching till they know how things are going with Jocelyn's writing. There isn't much trusting his talent in that, is there? When I think how Rob and I began . . . Still, I'd be glad to have them here if it weren't that . . .' Nina made some more mysterious passes with her hands. 'Oh, hell, I don't like trouble, Susan. I hate trouble.'

Susan gave her a puzzled look. 'What sort of trouble is there likely to be?'

'It's Annette,' Nina said. 'She kept Jocelyn on a string for ages and I've a feeling she's married him now only because she thinks he's going to be a success. She's calculating, predatory . . . But if I go on about her, you'll only think I'm jealous of her – which I am.' Nina gave a smile in which Susan thought, to her surprise, that there was a wry look of pain. 'Oh, never mind. One's a fool to parade that kind of feeling. And I'm wasting your time. Mine too. I've a load of things to do.'

She bent over the table, rapidly sorting out the papers on it, gave Susan some instructions about the work, promised to bring her a cup of coffee presently and left her.

Startled, because she had never before thought of Nina as a disappointed or unhappy woman, Susan quickly typed three lines, saw that she had made four mistakes in them, wrenched the paper out of the typewriter, crumpled it and hurled it at the wastepaper basket. After that she let her hands lie limply on the keyboard and stared at the door that Nina had closed behind her.

There was a grey emptiness in Susan's mind, a lack of feeling that surprised her. Yet with the shutting of the door the little room in which she now sat alone had abruptly changed into a frightening place, small and suffocating, a kind of trap from which it would be best to fly while she still could. It was as if the

25

anger against Jocelyn that had not yet flared up in her, the pain and the sense of betrayal that she was not yet feeling, were loose in the air, dangerous presences around her, like those that had seemed to throng the darkness when she was a child, when the light had just been turned out and the door closed behind her mother.

She gave a long sigh. Scraps of what Nina had said came back to her. '. . . confidential . . . Annette was giving him hell . . . these hush-hush things . . . a fool to parade that kind of feeling . . .'

They seemed to mean nothing. Susan rolled some more paper into the typewriter and began to pick letters out slowly and carefully. ' "Yes," said Porky Pye to Croc-the-Dile, "I'm just starting out on a very long journey. If you want to come with me . . ." '

She had been typing steadily for an hour when the door opened, letting in the fragrance of fresh coffee, and Rob Riscoe came in. He was holding a mug of coffee in his right hand, while on his gloved left fist he carried a great, golden-eyed goshawk.

The bird, whose leash was woven through Rob's gloved fingers, started to bate wildly at the sight of a stranger. Rob smiled at Susan, put the coffee down on the table near her, then quieted the bird, speaking to it softly until it was still and he could bring its head close to his and slide his cheek gently against it. A young bird, its first moult not quite over, it was not yet in its full splendour, though not many traces of its immature features remained among its new, shining, adult plumage.

There was a faint similarity in the features of the bird and the man. Rob's face was thin and aquiline, his eyes were a very light brown and very observant. He was a tall, spare man with a negligent stoop and dark hair streaked with grey. He wore a grey shirt and earth-stained flannel trousers. Susan could not remember ever to have seen him in any but the oldest clothes, yet, without knowing why, she had always felt confident that put away in some unvisited closet in the old house were expensive suits in which he would look extremely distinguished, if only he would wear them.

'You're a wonderful girl, Susan,' he observed. 'Nina says you came in and settled down to a session with our horrible Porky and his loathsome friends without a murmur of protest.'

Except that his eyes were on Susan, he might have been talking to the hawk, his voice remained so soothing and gentle, and no doubt the hawk thought that he was.

'I'm doing it dreadfully badly,' Susan answered. 'For some reason I can't concentrate this morning.'

'And who's to blame you?' He moved round behind her and bent and kissed her on the cheek, resting his free hand on her shoulder. 'Nina tells me she sprang our news on you as soon as you got here. The news about Jocelyn.'

Susan went very still under his hand. After a moment he withdrew it and moved away.

'Don't worry,' he said. 'Nina isn't observant. She'd no idea what a bombshell it was.'

There was another silence, then Susan said, 'As a matter of fact, Rob, it wasn't a bombshell. I'd heard it from Conrad Ives. The only thing is, I wasn't sure if it was true. Fiona and Arthur didn't seem to have heard anything about it. And if it was true, I wondered why it hadn't got into the papers. After all, that's Conrad's job, isn't it? Finding things out for his paper to print.'

'The *Swelsden Weekly Advertiser*? The news would have been crowded out by some hot stuff about the floral tributes sent to some town councillor's funeral. Apart from that, the lad may have principles of a sort. If he's told something in confidence, perhaps, like the rest of us, he only hands it on to his more intimate friends.' Rob propped a hip against a corner of the table. The goshawk, stirring a little, turned its head so that it could keep one flaming yellow eye on Susan. 'Does it still matter much to you, Susan? Somehow, I thought you were going to grow out of Jocelyn without too much difficulty.'

'I don't think I ever grow out of things very easily,' she answered.

Rob was gently caressing the breast of the hawk with the tip of a finger.

'I suppose I thought you would in this case because Jocelyn's

27

so damned easy to tread on. You can stamp him right into the ground and he doesn't complain. I'd have thought you'd have begun to like something a little more resistant.'

She made a helpless gesture with her hands. 'There are all sorts of different ways of being resistant.'

'How true – like getting married in secret, leaving it to Nina and me or Conrad Ives to break the news to you. Very tough-minded, that is. Shows great strength of character.'

Susan frowned. 'Don't, Rob. Please. Anyway, it isn't his getting married that's worrying me now. It was sure to happen some time, wasn't it? And I don't think I ever – ever honestly – thought it was going to be me. I just day-dreamed about it.'

'A little more than that, wasn't it?'

'Oh, I suppose it was. But now it's the thought of seeing him again so soon. . . . I don't know how it's going to feel. I know it's all finished, such as it was . . .' Suddenly she struck fiercely at the typewriter. 'Such as it was! And it wasn't anything! I was just a kid who got out of my depth and Jocelyn went to quite a lot of trouble steering me back to shore.'

'And then simply left you to dry out by yourself?'

'Wasn't that the best thing to do? I don't blame him at all, Rob. Do you understand that? Not for anything. Only the trouble is . . .'

'The trouble is,' Rob said as her words failed, 'it wasn't like that at all. Jocelyn was the one who was drowning and you did the rescuing. I've known my young brother a lot longer than you have.'

Susan grimaced at the page in front of her. The story of Porky Pye had reached a point when he and Croc-the-Dile and a few more friends were just starting out on a quest for an oracle called the Horse's Mouth, and so far the typing was good, but then came the line of angry gibberish with which Susan had relieved her feelings a moment ago. She slid the sheet out and added it to the other spoiled sheets in the wastepaper basket.

'You don't like Jocelyn, do you?' she said.

'I don't really know,' Rob replied. 'Perhaps not.'

'Then why did you offer him your cottage?'

'Well, there it was, an empty cottage and he happened to want one. And it was a good excuse for getting rid of the Taylors, who were a dead loss as neighbours. And whether or not I like Jocelyn, or he likes me, we're used to each other and get on pretty well. Do you like Fiona?'

'Yes, I suppose so. I think so. Yes, very much.'

'You're lucky, then. I can't imagine anything nicer than being able to like the members of one's own family. I detested my father, thought my mother a fool, and as you say, don't much like my brother. I imagine that's why I need my lovely Celia so much.' He smiled down at the hawk. 'All the same, Susan, however much you like Fiona, do you know what I'd do now if I were you?'

'What?'

'Clear out. At once. Before Jocelyn gets here.'

She picked a stub of pencil off the table and began to fiddle with it.

'I've been thinking about it,' she said. 'Only I've been thinking it might be better to wait until after I've seen him. I mean, I might find it's more or less over with me as well as with him.'

'But if you don't?'

She put her head a little on one side, looking up at Rob. She was wondering why she was talking to him like this. But she had always talked to him more than she intended and yet she was not even sure that she liked him. He had always scared her a little. For one thing, she found that, without thinking, she kept saying things to him which sometimes she had not said explicitly even to herself. Naturally that was frightening. It always left her with a feeling that he had a kind of power over her, could make her eat out of his hand if he wanted to, just as he could with that wild bird now perched so trustfully on his glove. For another thing, with those easy movements of his and that warm vitality, he had always had a strong physical effect upon her, which disturbed her because it seemed to her that there must be something all wrong about being moved in such a way by a man who was twenty years older than she was. Yet she had never found him trying to be anything but gentle, unalarming and perceptive.

'Rob, has that hawk ever turned on you and attacked you?' she asked abruptly. 'Has she ever tried to hurt you?'

He looked mildly surprised. 'Why should she? I've never done her any harm.'

'But suppose she just happened to feel like it all of a sudden.'

He shook his head. 'She won't. She needs me as much as I need her. We're working partners and as long as I don't upset the relationship by doing something stupid, she won't dream of turning on me. Of course, in the early stages it's different. When you're training a hawk you'd be a fool to give her the chance to get those great claws near your face. She could do you a lot of damage if she wanted to. Did Nina tell you, by the way, I've a new one promised to me, a falcon, a peregrine. I'm going away tomorrow to collect her.'

'That'll be exciting, won't it?' Susan said.

'Very exciting, though I'm not altogether sure it's a good idea. A peregrine needs open country, not the sort of woods we've got all round here. But I couldn't resist it when I heard that a friend of mine who's going abroad wanted someone to take on an eyas he'd just got hold of – that's a young bird taken from the nest, you know.'

Susan nodded. 'You'll have to go over to the downs to fly her. What are you going to call her?'

'Nina says I've got to call her Rosalind, to go with Celia. If you'd like to see something of her training, let me know. You'd find it extraordinarily fascinating.'

'May I? Really? Do you mean it?' In excitement at the thought, Susan momentarily forgot Jocelyn and all the problems connected with him.

'Of course, and welcome.' Rob got off the table. 'Now I'd better leave you in peace. You're staying to lunch, aren't you? I'll see you then.'

He went out and Susan returned to her typing.

They had lunch out of doors, a meal of cheese, salad, fruit, brown bread and cider. While they were eating, a mongrel tribe of barnyard fowls came around their feet, pecking for crumbs. The hens were unalarmed by the presence of Oliver, the Riscoes' elderly pointer, who investigated Susan with cautious sniffs, seemed to decide that he remembered her and rested his head on her knee, gazing up into her face. Yet when she started to stroke him, he began to snarl.

As she drew her hand away, Rob said, 'Don't worry, it only means he's loving it. He always snarls when he's happy. I've always believed it's because he grew up with a cat, an old and very domineering cat, with whom he had a furious love-hate relationship and naturally tried to copy as far as possible. I swear to you I've seen him trying to climb a tree after her. And when he snarls at someone for petting him, he's only trying to purr. Poor mixed-up old dog, he actually thinks he's a cat.'

'Rob!' Nina protested. She had been talking about the modern-ising of the Taylors' cottage that Jocelyn would have to do. 'Why do you talk such nonsense?'

'It isn't nonsense – is it, Susan?' he said. 'You'll have done some reading on animal behaviour. If a policeman can make a dog think it's a policeman and get it to help him catch murderers and such like, why shouldn't a cat be able to make the dog think it's a cat?'

So he led the talk away from human problems to less hurtful matters. Afterwards Susan returned to the study and went on typing.

She stopped at five o'clock. That was enough for the day, she thought. She sorted the typescript into neat piles, put the cover on the typewriter, stretched, yawned and got up.

It was only then that she became aware that the house was very quiet. Earlier there had been a sound of sawing and hammering made by Rob, who was constructing a perch for the peregrine falcon. There had been the whirring of the mowing machine as Nina cut the lawn round the house. There had been occasional whistling from Rob, sometimes taken up by Nina. But now there were neither voices nor other sounds of activity. As Susan went out into the passage she had the feeling that she had the house to herself.

She did not want simply to leave without telling either of the Riscoes that she was going. Standing at the bottom of the stairs she called out once or twice. When there was no answer, she went out into the garden and called again. As there was still no

31

answer, she went towards Rob's studio, which seemed the likeliest place in which to find him or Nina.

The studio was in an old barn that stood at right angles to the house. Celia, the goshawk, was on her perch in a shady spot, a few yards from the barn door. Near her on the grass was an inverted dustbin lid, filled with water, in which she could take a bath when she felt so inclined. She did not stir when Susan approached, except to move her head nervously. But Orlando, the eagle owl, who inhabited a big cage set against the wall of the studio, just by its door, glared wickedly at Susan, opened and closed his beak with a clopping sound and hissed. Returning his stare, Susan did her best to imitate his hiss. Her accent did not seem to impress him. He closed his eyes. Susan turned away to the open door of the studio.

It was a big, bare room that took up most of the barn. Its walls were of unplastered brick, whitewashed, and it was lit by two skylights set into the high roof which was supported by a framework of roughly hewn beams. The furniture was sparse. Besides the easel, the table, the one or two chairs and cupboards, the Anglepoise lamp on the table and the standard lamp that stood behind an old leather-covered armchair, there was only a row of Rob's charcoal sketches, unframed, pinned up at eye-level round the walls.

Some of the sketches were portraits of his friends. They were excellent likenesses, drawn with only a few lines. But far better than any of these were his drawings of the goshawk. Rob had caught all her moods, her quiet attentiveness when she was waiting for a hint of what was expected of her, her sudden furies, her triumph as she clutched her bleeding prey in her claws. Susan had often studied these drawings the year before and it had seemed to her that they expressed the strangest mixture of moods in Rob himself, moods of fierce admiration and of extraordinary tenderness and of something not far from hatred, but never of sentimentality. The killer instinct of the goshawk, which kills for the sake of killing and not only when it is hungry like the falcon, was never far from his mind.

Except for the skylights, there were no windows in the studio, but in one corner there was a door which led into the part of the barn where some of the Riscoes' other animals were kept, mainly the white rats and mice which they kept to provide fresh meat for their beloved birds of prey and which gave the whole place a faint, fusty, mousy odour.

Rob was not in the studio now, but Nina was. She was standing facing the far wall, with a piece of paper in her hand, at which she was staring. It looked, from where Susan stood, like one of Rob's drawings, which Nina apparently had just wrenched down from the wall. While Susan watched in astonishment, Nina tore the paper in half. Then she tore it in half again, then into smaller and smaller fragments. All the time she chattered to herself frantically, wildly and incoherently.

Susan stood staring at her stupidly. Last year, somewhere near to where Nina was standing, there had hung a picture of Susan herself. But it could not, it surely could not be this that now lay scattered in little pieces on the floor . . .

Turning swiftly, Susan ran away.

3

The evening was still sunny. There was a scent of meadowsweet in the lane. The removal van, of course, had gone from the end of it and already the cottage had the lost, blind look that comes to empty buildings.

What made Susan stop when she reached it she did not know. She had had no thought of stopping there when she left the farmhouse. Yet at the gate she stood still, looked round uncertainly and went in.

Pausing half-way up the path, she surveyed the garden. It was a long, long time since it had had any attention. A few potato plants sprouted among weeds. Dead cabbage stalks stood up crookedly in the middle of clumps of willowherb. Thick mats of bindweed smothered the currant bushes. By the door of the cottage there was a pile of rubbish. There were old cardboard cartons, empty bottles, decaying sacks. There was a bucket with a hole through the bottom and a broom with a broken handle.

Susan went on and tried the door. Naturally, it was locked.

Still not understanding what was driving her, she wandered round the cottage, not furtively, exactly, yet with a strong feeling that she had no right to be there. Looking in at a window, she saw a dingy parlour, papered with a faded pattern of cabbage roses. From the kitchen window she saw a cracked sink and a dripping tap, in the bathroom a rust-streaked bath and curtains of cobwebs.

Suddenly she felt nervous. What was she going to say if she came face to face with Jocelyn Riscoe all of a sudden?

To do that, to be caught peeping into his house like a spy, would be rather more than she could bear. Furthermore, she had not yet prepared a face or a sentence with which to greet him when they had to meet. And unprepared, heaven knew what she might do or say. She walked quickly away down the path and on along the road to her sister's home.

At dinner that evening Arthur announced, 'Our python is still growing. A conservative estimate now is that it's fifteen foot long. By the weekend I think we can count on its being a twenty foot reptile and very fearsome and dangerous to meet in the dark.'

'So you've been to the Dragon again,' Fiona said. 'It's a nightly exercise.'

Arthur smiled as he went on carving. 'I must keep my finger on the pulse of public opinion in this time of crisis. The curious thing is, there was really a quite panicky atmosphere in the place. Everyone kept saying that of course he personally wasn't scared, yet they simply couldn't keep off the subject. And they were surprisingly abusive about the Riscoes, not merely for letting the python get away, you know, but for having it around at all. They implied it was just the lunatic sort of thing you could expect the Riscoes to do and that it was time someone told them what people were thinking about them.' He handed Susan an immense helping of roast duck. 'Too much?' he said when she protested. 'No, no, it can't possibly be too much for a growing girl. You eat it up.'

'Darling,' Fiona said, 'Susan isn't a growing girl any more. She's twenty-one. You'd better split that helping between us.'

He shook his head dubiously, but moved some slices of the duck and the stuffing on to another plate.

'Well, as I was saying,' he went on, 'I was rather astonished at the degree of antagonism to the Riscoes. I thought they were popular.'

'I don't believe anyone's popular in that pub the moment his back's turned,' Fiona said. 'I expect they dropped the Riscoes as soon as you left and had a good chew on our bones.'

'That's different, at least I sincerely hope it is,' he said, 'because this wasn't just the usual guffawing over the Riscoes' eccentricities, or any of the old familiar scandals, like the one last year about Nina and Jocelyn that caused so much enjoyment. That sort of thing is actually quite a tribute. It's a proof that a person is contributing his share to his neighbours' entertainment. No, this was – well, quite soberly resentful.'

'It's all right, it'll all die down as soon as they find the python,' Fiona said.

'Then I hope they find it soon and that in the meantime it hasn't swallowed anybody's dear little dog or squealing baby.'

Fiona looked genuinely shocked. 'Don't!' she said.

'My dear, that's the sort of thing they were saying. The atmosphere was nasty. Genuinely nasty.' He helped himself to some new potatoes. 'Are these out of the garden?'

'Of course. But they – those people – they can't believe—' Fiona looked at Susan. 'There isn't any real danger, is there?'

Susan gave a start and looked at her blankly. Since Arthur had dropped his extraordinary remark about Nina and Jocelyn her mind had wandered away, not to start thinking actively about what he had said, but simply to take refuge in a kind of vacancy. Nina and Jocelyn? Nina, Jocelyn . . . ? The absurdity of it, the utter incredibility!

'Susan, there isn't any real danger from the python, is there?' Fiona said, raising her voice a little.

'What? – Oh, to babies and things,' Susan answered absently. 'I told you, I don't know anything about pythons.'

Fiona gave her a puzzled look, then exchanged glances with her husband. He gave a faint shrug of his shoulders and added a big spoonful of peas to Susan's plate, as if he felt sure that large quantities of good fresh food were obviously badly needed by her.

Susan went up to her room immediately after dinner, picked up Brachet's *Biochemical Embryology* and doggedly set herself to read. But she kept on seeing Nina's face, frantic and tear-stained, as it had been when she had stood, tearing up the drawing in Rob's studio. The thought of going back to the farmhouse tomorrow seemed horrible, even if Nina did not know that she had been seen, betraying herself so dreadfully. But there was still all that typing that Susan had promised to do . . .

It was very gloomily that she set off next day along the lane. She found Nina bewilderingly her normal self. She was talkative and cheerful, rushing energetically from job to job. Rob was away, she told Susan as she let her in. He had driven off early to fetch the peregrine falcon.

'Did you know a peregrine's a go-up in the world for us?' Nina said, laughing. 'There are very strict class distinctions in falconry, at least there were in the Middle Ages. Emperors had eagles, kings had gyrfalcons, peregrines were for the nobility and the goshawk was what the mere yeoman had, which happened to suit him pretty well, because a goshawk is much the best for the lowly job of filling the pot – in fact, they've sometimes been called kitchen hawks. But Rob says it's every falconer's ambition to fly a long-wing. They're so enchantingly beautiful and they go in for such glorious aerobatics, just for the fun of it. You can understand the fascination. Well, I'll see you later. D'you know, those damned people in the cottage went off yesterday without returning the key? They were supposed to bring it along before they left, but they just haven't bothered. It's lucky we've got a spare one for Jocelyn.' She whisked out of the room.

Susan pulled her chair up to the table, arranged the pile of manuscript and started typing.

That day she left at about the same time as the day before, but this time saw Nina in the kitchen garden, busily picking raspberries. She waved cheerfully without straightening her back, called out, 'Bless you, Susan, you're saving my life! See you on Monday,' and went on picking.

Susan found it difficult to believe that that scene in the studio yesterday had ever happened.

This evening she walked straight past the cottage without stopping, but as soon as she had passed the gate she heard her name being called from the doorway. Standing stock-still for a moment, she turned half reluctantly and saw that a man was standing at the open door.

'Oh, it's you,' she said, her excitement dying.

Conrad Ives came loping along the path towards her, pulled the gate open, put an arm round her and kissed her briefly but hard. He was about her own age and was small and slight with fair hair, a pale freckled face, surprised-looking sandy eyebrows and a way of carrying his head thrust forward which gave him the appearance of crouching slightly, of being ready to spring at whatever had caught his interest.

'Well, wasn't I right?' he said, letting Susan go without appearing to be disconcerted by her unresponsiveness. 'The Taylors have gone and Jocelyn Riscoe's moving in. Have you been inside the place? It's fascinating. It gives you the feeling that anything could happen there, absolutely anything, and that that's what it's for, you know.'

Susan gave him a chilling look. 'What d'you mean, *for*? It isn't *for* anything except for people to live in.'

'Oh yes, it is, it's a setting, it's a background for some strange and dramatic event. That's why I've been keeping my eye on it. Something's certain to happen here.'

'If you've really been keeping an eye on it, I should think it's because you haven't enough else to do,' Susan said. 'Why d'you stay on on that absurd paper, Conrad? It's a fearful waste of time.'

'I've told you, I believe journalism's a job that it's best to start at the bottom,' he said.

'Does it have to be rock bottom?'

'You academic snobs,' he remarked pleasantly. 'How you live and die in ignorance.'

'Anyway, how did you get in?' she asked.

'Walked in. Nothing to stop me.' He was holding the gate open, expecting Susan to come in.

Walking up the path with him, she said, 'I suppose you were simply keeping an eye on the Taylors. Why can't you just say so instead of talking nonsense about strange and dramatic events?'

'Of course I was keeping an eye on them,' he said. 'Naturally. So was everyone. But that doesn't mean the other thing I said was nonsense. Far from it. Come and take a look round. It'll give you the creeps.'

He pushed open the door that he had half-closed behind him when he came out of the cottage.

The door opened straight into the small front room into which Susan had peered yesterday. It was not as dark as she had thought from outside, but it was even dirtier. The rose-patterned wallpaper was flyblown and faded, except where the pictures had hung and the furniture stood that had belonged to the old couple who had lived there for half a century before the Taylors moved in. They had been a farm labourer and his wife who at last had gone their different ways, he to the village churchyard, she to a married daughter's council house in Swelsden and then to the crematorium there.

Susan walked through the room to the kitchen and tried to turn off the dripping tap over the greasy sink, but the tap went on slowly dripping. She looked into the primitive bathroom that opened out of the kitchen, having been built on to the cottage only ten years or so ago. There was a high-water mark of crusted dirt round the rusted bath, the floor was of bare boards and there was a dank insanitary smell. Conrad did not follow her, but looking at her expectantly when she returned to the sitting-room, said, 'I was right, wasn't I?'

'But I don't suppose you ever found out anything important about the Taylors, did you?' she asked.

'I found out far more than most people. Poor Sandra, d'you know she used to sit here and cry by the hour? How many people knew that, d'you think?'

'How did you find out?'

It was odd, normally Susan hardly noticed such things as dust and cobwebs, her sister's domestic perfectionism striking her as faintly funny; yet here she was, noticing everything, the dead flies along the window-sill, the squashed cigarette-ends on the floor, the mustiness and the feeling of chill with which the air seemed saturated, in spite of the day-long sunshine. Was Jocelyn really going to live here?

'We talked a few times in the Dragon,' Conrad said, 'and I got interested in the set-up. There was something so obviously wrong about Taylor. I got the idea he was hiding out here after committing some sort of crime – a pay-snatch, or something like that. So I tried to take a picture of him but unluckily he caught on and nearly smashed the camera and after that Sandra wouldn't talk to me any more. He never let her talk to anyone if he could help it. The poor kid was half-crazy with loneliness and boredom. No offence to your sister or the Riscoes, but she could

39

have gone out of her mind without anyone bothering. She ought to be grateful to me because I've a feeling it was the way I started to hang around that made them move off.'

'The things you feel, Conrad!' Susan began to laugh. 'This pay-snatch, for instance. Have you any evidence it ever happened, or did you invent it this moment?'

'It may not have been a pay-snatch,' he answered seriously. 'He may have smuggled heroin or murdered his landlady in Clapham, I don't know. He'd done something, though, and he was in hiding.'

'But what did you hope to find here today? You didn't think they'd leave anything incriminating behind, did you?'

'Oh, I was just nosing around. I was really on my way to the Riscoes to see if I could pick up anything new about this python that's got loose. Why not come along with me, Susan, and see what we can find out? Then we might go on and have a drink at the Dragon.'

'No, thank you,' she said, 'I've been typing for Nina all day. She's seen enough of me.'

'All right then, let's just have the drink. Come on, I've got the bike in the lane.'

'No, Fiona's expecting me home for dinner.'

'I only said for a drink. We shan't be gone all night.'

'Nina'll give you a drink and bring you up to date about the python too – though I should have thought everyone's got tired of hearing about it by now.'

'Don't you believe it!' Conrad said. 'The story's only getting started. Do you know that a certain Mrs Pike in the village lost her Pekinese dog and thinks the python got it? And that a Mr Smiley, returning home after his usual pint – as he put it – saw an enormous snake hanging like a noose from the branch of a tree and if he hadn't very cleverly gone flat on his face on the ground where it couldn't reach him, it would certainly have strangled him?'

'I suppose that's meat and drink to the *Swelsden Weekly Advertiser*,' Susan said, 'or could be if you hadn't just made it all up.' She walked to the door. 'Conrad, was this key here in the lock like this when you came in?'

He glanced at the key in the rickety lock of the front door.

'It must have been,' he said. 'I didn't notice.'

Susan took the key out of the lock.

'If you're going to see Nina,' she said as they both went out-side, 'you might give it to her. The Taylors were supposed to take it along to her yesterday but they didn't bother.'

He pocketed the key. 'All right. But you're wrong about my making those things up, Susan. As it happens, I haven't much imagination. I'm just extremely observant. Sure you won't change your mind about the drink?'

'Quite sure.'

'You might at least say you're sorry.'

'I'm sorry.'

'I wonder why I like you,' he said. 'It's something of an enigma really. Goodbye now.'

'Goodbye.'

She waited until the sound of his motor bike had faded up the lane, then walked on slowly to the Lasletts' house.

She was nearly there before it occurred to her that since the cottage had been locked when she had looked into it the evening before, yet had been open today, the key that she had given to Conrad could hardly be the one that the Taylors had had, unless perhaps they had returned for some reason later in the evening. More probably, however, it was the spare key that Nina had mentioned to Susan. Nina must have gone to the cottage to take a look round some time during the day while Susan was typing and left the key behind by mistake. If that were so, she should be glad to have it returned by Conrad and also to have someone to whom to give a drink and to talk to while Rob was away.

There had been times when Susan herself had enjoyed a drink with Conrad and been able to listen with amusement to his fantasies and exaggerations. But that had been before Jocelyn's telephone calls and visits had started to grow fewer, and then had altogether stopped, and she had not yet grown irritated with Conrad because he simply failed to fill a gap.

Next morning Jocelyn moved into the cottage.

By arrangement with Nina, because it was Saturday, Susan had stayed with the Lasletts instead of going to Bright's Farm to go

41

on with her typing. From her bedroom window she saw the furniture van go up the lane, as the other van had when the Taylors were leaving. She saw it stop at the cottage gate and Jocelyn come out to meet the men who climbed down from the van. She saw them start to carry the furniture in and Jocelyn go in and out, giving directions. She saw him take a walk round the garden, smoking a cigarette, his dark head bent as he surveyed the wilderness of weeds. For a few minutes she felt petrified, unable to leave the window, but then turned away to her table, spread out her notes and started reading.

At twelve o'clock Fiona came into the room.

'You know, I can't get over your having become such a glutton for work,' she said, after watching Susan for a moment. 'It's very impressive. Such a pity it'll all be wasted, but it's the taxpayers' money, so who cares?'

Susan went on staring at her book with her head in her hands. 'Why wasted?'

'Because you'll get married some time soon and never give science another thought.'

'That doesn't sound very likely.'

'You wait and see,' Fiona said. 'I never imagined I'd settle down happily into being the perfect housewife in the suburbs of a place like Swelsden. I'd made up my mind to have lots of lovers with glamorous jobs, who'd take me travelling all over the world. But look at me now, married to Arthur, who somehow manages to give me everything I really seem to want in life. Of course, I haven't got your brains.'

Susan pushed her hair back from her face. She had a headache and her eyes were smarting. Was she beginning to need spectacles, she wondered.

'I haven't met an Arthur yet,' she said politely. 'Anyway, I don't want to get married yet. I want – I think I want to understand more about other people first. I used not to worry about that, but now I keep thinking that I don't know anything.'

'Then for God's sake, why keep your nose stuck in those books all day? That isn't the way to learn.'

Susan laughed. 'They're nice books, Fiona. Awfully nice books. I *like* reading them.'

42

'Have it your own way.' Fiona laughed too. Crossing to the window, she looked out. 'I suppose the Riscoes told you who's moving into the cottage. It's Rob's brother, Jocelyn. That ought to be an improvement on the Taylors – though I've just been over to ask him to lunch and you never saw such battered old furniture in your life, it's really no better than the Taylors'. You'd never think it belonged to a man with a successful play running in London. There's a desk with cigarette burns all over the top and the most awful electric cooker, hundreds of years old. And the linoleum! You'd think he'd have left it behind, wherever it came from. But there he was, down on his hands and knees, laying it in the bathroom – terrible stuff, pitted all over, as if someone had been trampling it in hob-nailed boots. And I sat down in an easy-chair and one of the springs jabbed right into me. It's nothing to do with me, of course, but it doesn't strike me as natural. I mean, he *is* making a lot of money out of that play, isn't he?'

'I expect it all goes in taxes.' Susan had not joined Fiona at the window. 'Did you say he's coming to lunch?'

'No, I said I went over to ask him. I thought it might be a help to him while's he's settling in. His wife isn't here yet. But he's having lunch with the Riscoes, or rather with Nina. Rob's away.' Fiona gave another laugh. 'His wife must be a brave woman, considering all the talk there was about Jocelyn and Nina last year. But perhaps she doesn't know about it.'

'There was nothing to know!' Susan's voice rang out sharply and suddenly there were red patches on her cheeks.

'Oh, my dear, you'd never have noticed, even if it was happening right under your nose,' Fiona said. 'You were so completely wrapped up in Rob. I expect you've forgotten it by now, but you never stopped talking about him – Rob this and Rob that all day. Arthur used to laugh about it, but you had me worried, because actually Rob's rather awful with women.'

'Rob?' Susan said. 'You thought I was in love with *Rob*?'

'And no wonder. He's extremely attractive in that relaxed sort of come-and-cry-on-my-shoulder way of his. And I love him dearly myself. But he's got no scruples whatever.'

'How d'you know?'

'By using my instincts.'

'Is that all you used?'

Fiona gave her a thoughtful look. 'D'you know, Susan, that's one of the first really catty remarks I've heard from you for a very long time. Are you by any chance beginning to grow up, my child?'

'But it's all so stupid!' Susan's face was stormy. 'I simply don't understand how people can be so stupid. Nobody seems to know anything about what's going on in anyone else. You were quite wrong about me, you know. I liked Rob all right, but it was – it was Celia, the goshawk, that fascinated me. And you're wrong about Jocelyn and Nina too – I know you're wrong. And I expect you're wrong about Rob, I don't believe he's in the least unscrupulous with women, or if he is, I don't see what business it is of yours.'

'All right, I'm wrong, I'm wrong about everything. Only don't say you haven't been warned. You're a lot older than you were a year ago, and a lot better-looking – and don't look so furious, it's perfectly true, and if I were you I'd enjoy it while you can instead of getting bogged down in those awful books and pining after a man who's twice your age. Now what do you say to driving over to the sea this afternoon for a bathe?'

The coast was only twenty miles away, not a very interesting stretch of it, low-lying and pebbly, but usually not too crowded and sufficiently pleasant for a swim on a hot afternoon. Last year Fiona and Susan had often driven over to swim and sunbathe.

Susan paid no attention to the question. She was bewildered and extraordinarily angry with Fiona. Turning back to the books and papers on the table, she muttered, 'It's all a silly mess. There's absolutely no sense in anything you've said.'

'Have you brought your swimming things?' Fiona went on patiently. 'Arthur comes home for lunch today. He'll be able to come too. Shall we go? Would you like it?'

'All right,' Susan grunted.

'Come and help me with lunch then. It's such a glorious day, I think we'll have it out in the garden. You can carry some of the things out for me.'

She went downstairs.

44

Susan got up and started to wander nervously about the room, but after a few minutes followed Fiona.

But they did not go to the sea that afternoon.

While they were at lunch in the garden Mr Burke, the village constable who had first brought them the news of the python's escape, appeared round the corner of the house. He had come to tell them that police from Swelsden, with dogs, were coming over that afternoon to search for the python in the woods and fields in the neighbourhood.

There had been complaints, he said, concerning a lost Pekinese and a budgerigar that had disappeared in mysterious circumstances. And that morning a young child had come running home, screaming, after having had some fearful fright in the wood. The police wanted the Lasletts' permission to search their garden too. Arthur readily gave the permission and then became so interested in the search and how it was to be organised that in the end he succeeded in being invited to join the search party.

Fiona, disgusted at losing his company for the afternoon, said nothing more about the swim. She and Susan stayed in the garden, lying in deck chairs in the shade, hearing the occasional barking of dogs in the woods and now and then catching a glimpse of a uniformed figure among the trees.

The furniture van had driven away from the cottage and the cottage door had closed on Jocelyn Riscoe. No doubt he had much to do. He did not come to join in the search.

The police did not find the python.

But in the late afternoon, when the shadows were lengthening and the midges were coming out to dance in clouds like wavering mist, and the dogs had grown bored and the police tired, they found, in the midst of a patch of brambles, the dead body of a young girl with yellow hair.

4

Conrad Ives brought the news to Susan and Fiona.

He had spent most of the afternoon roaming the woods with the police and had been almost on the spot when a shout had gone up from a thicket and the men who were nearest had come running, expecting to find the python.

They had found Sandra Taylor. She was wearing the short black dress in which Susan had seen her wandering about the cottage garden while the furniture was being loaded on to the van. There were scratches on the girl's face and sticks and leaves in her yellow hair. These had come, it was evident, from her body having been dragged through the undergrowth, not from a struggle in the wood, of which there were no signs.

She had been strangled. But there was no mark of a cord round her neck. It was a strong pair of hands that had killed her.

'They don't know how long ago it happened,' Conrad said. He had flung himself down on the grass at Susan's feet. His face was whiter than usual, with the freckles standing out like little flecks of mud all over it. 'They think she's been dead at least twenty-four hours and the chances are it happened in the cottage after the removal people left, unless it was the men in the van who did it. Did you see the van, Mrs Laslett? D'you know whose it was?'

'I saw it,' Susan said. 'The name on it was something like Wells or Willis.'

'West,' Fiona said. 'R. J. West from Swelsden. It was one of their vans.'

Conrad jumped to his feet. 'Thanks, Mrs Laslett. The police will want to know that.'

He went running off towards the wood.

Susan kept a wide-eyed gaze upon him till he vanished among the trees.

'What kind of people are R. J. West?' she asked.

'An old firm. A very good firm. They've been there ages.' Fiona's voice was thin and high. She sat bolt-upright on the edge of her chair. 'Everybody knows them. It couldn't be them.'

'Then it was Taylor. He must have come back.'

'No, it wasn't Taylor – not if she was strangled – like that.'

'Why not?'

'Because he's got a withered right arm. He couldn't strangle anybody.'

'Then—' But Susan really had nothing to say. Her impulse to talk was only to drive away her memory of having gone up to the cottage door and found it locked, although a day later Conrad had said that he had found it unlocked.

'It must have been a tramp,' Fiona said.

'Yes, of course.' Only why should a tramp bother with locking and unlocking doors, and if it was in the cottage that he had killed Sandra, why hadn't he simply left her body there instead of dragging it across the lane and through the wood into the brambles? Hesitantly, Susan suggested, 'If Taylor came back with a friend . . . '

'Oh, for God's sake!' Fiona cried shrilly, jumping up from her chair. 'You don't know anything. I don't know anything. What's the point of making silly guesses? Arthur!' He was not in sight, but she ran towards the wood, calling him. 'Arthur!'

At the sound of her voice a policeman appeared at the point where Conrad had just disappeared and turned her back, walking to the house with her.

'Mr Laslett's talking to Inspector Piggott,' the policeman said. 'They'll be coming here shortly. Meanwhile I'd keep away if I was you, Mrs Laslett. It isn't a pretty thing to see.'

'No,' Fiona said. 'Yes. I mean . . . ' She had started to cry. As the man returned to the wood she exclaimed, 'Come inside, Susan! I can't stand it out here any longer!'

Susan was not much surprised. Fiona had never had much fortitude in a crisis. She had always cried readily. Presently she would pull herself together and no one would be able to guess then, from her calm exterior, how emotionally she had reacted at first. With Susan it was always the other way round, an ominous calm to begin with and later a tempest.

They went into the sitting-room and Fiona closed the french windows behind them, to make the sounds from the wood less audible. Walking up and down the room, the tears still running down her cheeks, she said, 'Oh God, I love this place so much! The garden, the house, everything. I love it so, Susan. Which is strange, isn't it, when you think of the sort of things I used to like when I was younger? Do you remember the crazy sort of things I used to do? Poor Daddy was certain I was going to the devil. It was all so innocent really, just feckless and restless and unstable, because I hadn't found a man I really cared for . . . ' She stood still, peering uncertainly through the blur of her tears at Susan. 'Why am I talking about this? I suppose because I'm afraid I'll never be able to feel the same about the place again.'

Susan, still outwardly quiet, was feeling sick and shivery. She found it difficult to speak. 'I don't see why not,' she said. 'It isn't as if . . . '

'It isn't as if what? What are you thinking about?' Fiona glared at her. 'You don't look as if you've realised what's happened.'

'I was going to say, it isn't as if she was someone you really knew – or cared for – or was murdered here, actually in this house.'

'No. No, of course not. Didn't Conrad say it happened in the cottage?'

'Jocelyn's and Annette's.'

'Yes, but it can't mean as much to them. They needn't stay here. Why should they? They can't have any feelings about the place yet. They haven't put down roots. And it's a horrid house, anyway.'

'Their first home . . . ' As Susan said it she suddenly had a curious new feeling, a sympathy, a sense of fellowship in disaster with Jocelyn which made her wonder why she had been so afraid all day of having sooner or later to come face to face with him. The thought of him alone in his outraged home, a place desecrated by horror, now made her want to run over there as fast as she could to help him somehow, even if it was only by washing up crockery, scrubbing floors or hanging pictures. She would do anything that might help him to blot out the image of what must have happened in one of the empty rooms. She made a hurried, almost unconscious movement towards the door.

'Where are you going?' Fiona asked quickly.

'Out,' Susan said.

'You can't. That inspector's going to want to see you when he gets here.'

'Why should he?'

'He'll want to see us all. He'll ask you about the van and the girl and everything else you saw that morning.'

Susan sank on to the long black sofa.

'Yes, of course. She was so excited, you know. She wanted so to go to London. I wonder if—'

But that was when Arthur came in, accompanied by Detective-Inspector Piggott and a young sergeant.

The inspector was a burly, grey-haired man of about fifty, with a lined face and faded-looking blue eyes which never lingered long on the face of anyone to whom he was talking, or revealed much interest in anything else either. It was as if they had already seen too much of the world around him and grown very weary of their work. The sergeant, on the other hand, far from appearing tired of observing the passing scene, seemed only to find difficulty in deciding which it would be the more rewarding to watch, Fiona or Susan.

'I won't take up much of your time, Mrs Laslett,' Inspector Piggott said in a low, flat voice, 'but your husband tells me you saw this man Taylor leave the evening before the van came for the furniture. Is that right?'

'Yes,' Fiona said. 'My sister and I were looking out of the window and we saw him put some suitcases into his car and drive off. Mr Burke, the constable, saw it too. He was going round the village, telling people about the python's escape from Bright's Farm. He spoke to Mr Taylor just as he was leaving.'

'Can you tell me anything more about it, anything that struck you specially?' the inspector asked.

Fiona shook her head. 'I don't think so. He just put the suitcases into the car and drove away.'

49

'And you didn't see him come back later, or think you heard the car.'

'No,' she said. 'Why? Do you think he did?'

The faded blue eyes eluded hers. 'It was merely an inquiry. The girl was killed by manual strangulation, for which two hands are needed. But Taylor, I've been told, has a withered arm. So it seems unlikely that he can be the murderer. All the same, if he'd returned that evening or next day it would be of interest, especially if by any chance he didn't come alone.'

'I saw something,' Susan said abruptly.

They all turned their heads to look at her except the sergeant, who happened to be looking at her already.

'I saw her dancing – the girl – after he'd gone,' she said.

'*Dancing?*' Arthur spoke with a startled air, as if Susan had just incomprehensibly changed the subject.

But there was no surprise in Inspector Piggott's faded blue eyes. It would take a great deal more than that to surprise him.

'Yes?' he said.

'In the cottage,' Susan said. 'I saw her through the window from my bedroom. She was waving her arms and spinning round and round. She looked simply wild with delight. I've been wondering if it was delight that Taylor had gone.'

'That's an interesting idea,' the inspector said, as if in fact he found it no more interesting than a report on the weather. 'You mean, of course, that she'd no intention of following him to London.'

'I think she was going to London,' Susan said. 'Next morning we talked for a few minutes over the garden fence and she seemed terrifically excited at the idea of going. She said she was going to get a job and a lot of new clothes and she talked as if she meant to rejoin Taylor. But it didn't sound as if she liked him much. She seemed to be angry with him for having kept her here where she never saw anybody and couldn't wear the nice clothes she'd bought when she first went off with him.'

'That's interesting, very interesting,' the inspector said. 'Because it could mean she was expecting someone else to pick her up. Did she say why Taylor left the day before?'

'She said he'd gone on ahead to get the new place ready.'

'Did she say where the new place was?'

'No,' she said.

His gaze strayed round the room, fastening on the abstract painting above the fireplace as if that at least were something on which he could count not to make any tiresome demand for understanding.

'Did it strike you as odd,' he asked, 'that the man should go on ahead like that, leaving such a very young girl to manage all by herself at this end?'

Susan shook her head. As a very young girl she had often been left to manage things by herself. 'I didn't think about it. Perhaps it was.'

'Inspector,' Fiona said, 'the removal van was one of R. J. West's. They'll be able to tell you where the furniture was to be delivered.'

'Yes, and whether or not it was the arrangement that the girl was to go with the van. That's done for the customer sometimes.' He transferred his weary gaze to Fiona. 'Have you ever seen any visitors at the cottage, Mrs Laslett? Do you know anything about the Taylors' friends?'

'I don't think they had any here,' she answered. 'I never saw anybody visit them.'

Arthur said, 'They sometimes went to the pub, the Dragon, but even then they sat by themselves in the lounge bar and never spoke to anyone. I sometimes thought the girl looked as if she'd like to mix with the other people there, but Taylor always managed to put a stop to it.'

'This man Taylor, can you describe him?' Inspector Piggott asked.

'Go on, Fiona,' Arthur said, 'you're much better at describing people than I am.'

'Well, I think he was about thirty-seven or -eight,' she said, 'and about five foot ten. He'd darkish hair that hung over his collar and he always wore terribly pointed black shoes and tight trousers. He was thin and narrow shouldered and he'd that withered right arm. And he didn't seem to go away anywhere to work but spent most of his time loafing around doing nothing. He and the girl used to drive into Swelsden now and then to do

51

their shopping and once or twice I think he went away for a few days. . . .' She gave an embarrassed smile. 'I know what you're thinking, Inspector. Well, I did snoop. There was something so wrong about them, I couldn't help it.'

'Most fortunately,' he replied in a voice without expression. 'That description should make it very easy for us to find him. But did he never tell anyone anything at all about where they'd come from?'

'Not that I ever heard,' she said. 'I don't know if the Riscoes know a little more about him than we do. Taylor may have given them references when he rented the cottage.'

'Though if he did,' Arthur said, 'I should think they were probably forged.'

Inspector Piggott got up to go. 'Possibly. It's also possible that we've got his picture in our files. I might ask you later to come into Swelsden to see if you can identify him, Mrs Laslett. Apart from that, I hope I shan't have to trouble you much any more.'

'Anything we can do . . .' Arthur said as he saw the two policemen out to the road.

When he returned to the sitting-room Fiona flew into his arms, clung to him and began to cry again. Between her sobs she said she was so sorry she was being such a fool, but she couldn't help it.

Arthur stroked her hair absently, looking past her at Susan.

'Susan, Rob's away, isn't he?' he asked.

'Yes,' she said.

'Do you know when he's coming back?'

'No, I don't think Nina said anything about that.'

'She's alone there then. Perhaps we ought to ask her over here for the night.'

Fiona, with her face still pressed against his shoulder, answered, 'She isn't alone. Jocelyn's there.'

'Oh, yes,' he said, 'I was forgetting.'

'You – you don't think the murderer's hanging around still, do you?' she asked.

'We don't know, do we?'

'No . . .' She dabbed at her eyes. 'All right, I'll telephone and see how she feels.'

But Nina, on the telephone, was surprisingly breezy. She seemed less upset by the murder of the girl in the wood than she would have been if Celia, the goshawk, had escaped or had had a fit, as hawks sometimes do, when Rob was not there to deal with it. Nina was extremely loquacious, however, as she always was on the telephone, and Fiona was held captive by it for the next twenty minutes, in the middle of which Susan slipped quietly out of the house and walked along the road to the cottage.

There were police cars in the road, with one or two uniformed men standing about. Beyond them was an ambulance. The men turned steady stares on Susan as she paused, but did not speak to her. The cottage door was wide open.

She went up to it, put her head in and called 'Jocelyn!'

He came swiftly out of the kitchen. He was in a soiled shirt with his sleeves rolled up and a pair of paint-flecked flannel trousers. His dark hair was ruffled and there was a smear of paint on one cheek. Because usually he was neatly and soberly dressed, it made him resemble Rob more than usual, a slighter, smaller Rob, handsome in the hawk-faced Riscoe way, but with a look of intensity about him that the easygoing Rob had never possessed, and at the same time a diffidence, a kind of shyness that had always made him appear far younger than he was. Jocelyn was thirty-five, the same age as Nina.

His face lit up when he saw Susan. He put out both hands to grasp her by the shoulders. But it happened that in one hand he was holding a great knife. Its blade glittered as it came towards her.

At her startled look, he tossed the knife aside.

'Sorry,' he said. 'I've just been sharpening it. I took the edge off it this morning, laying some linoleum in the bathroom. The floor there is all splinters. Come in. I've been wondering when I'd see you.'

He drew her into the room.

It had already changed a good deal since Susan had been in it the day before. The cobwebs and dead flies had been swept away, the floor had been scrubbed, and the musty smell had been dispelled by the pleasanter odours of soap and of the fresh white paint that covered one wall. Under this first coat the cabbage roses were only pale, ghostly presences.

Some furniture was stacked under a dust-sheet in the middle of the room. Jocelyn dragged a chair out from under the sheet and thrust Susan into it. He remained standing himself, smiling down at her.

'You don't know how good it is to see you,' he said. 'It makes things feel almost sane again. You know what's supposed to have happened in here, don't you?'

'Was it really in here – in this room?' Susan asked. She wondered at herself for feeling so calm, so natural with him, and so amazingly glad to see him.

'Or somewhere in the cottage,' he answered. 'It's why I had to stop painting the walls, or doing much else either. The police are coming back to do a lot more investigating, dusting for finger-prints and so on, though I've probably obliterated everything already that might have been useful. I've been scrubbing and painting ever since I got here last night.'

'You didn't sleep here without any furniture!'

'No, I slept up at the farm, but I did get a little cleaning up done before it got too dark.'

'I came over to ask if I could help,' Susan said.

'That was a nice thought. But I'm pretty much held up until the police finish. How about tomorrow, though? If your offer stands, I could do with a strong girl to do some fetching and carrying.'

'All right.'

He slid a hand over her hair, ruffling it. He had always liked to touch her hair.

'Only if you've nothing else to do,' he said. 'It may be a waste of effort, in any case. After what's happened I don't see Annette agreeing to live here. She's been dubious about it all along. She doesn't think I ought to have given up teaching on the strength of one moderately successful play. She loves teaching herself. She's brilliant at it. She can do anything she likes with children. So she's never been able to understand why I hate it. But if you only knew how I hate it, Susan!'

He gave a wry laugh and deliberately repressed the excitement in his voice.

'I like children – I think I do – but strictly one or two or even three at a time. Not sixty! Think of it. Think of having to stand up in front of sixty scrubbed, wooden faces, all staring at you like a lot of bullocks over a gate, and of having to try to light some sort of spark in all those empty eyes. I used to get ill just thinking about it. And if you knew how I envied Rob. To have started off in the R.A.F. – did you know he'd done that? Naturally, he'd the makings of a wonderful pilot, the cool head, the right amount of self-confidence and not a nerve in his body. He loved it so, he was going into civil flying when he'd finished his service. But he dropped it when he and Nina got married because they chanced on a way of making a living that he liked even better than flying, because it made him able to live just the life he wanted . . .' He stopped himself again. 'I'm sorry, I always talk too much when I see you. You actually listen to what one says, or you manage to look as if you do.'

'What made you make up your mind to drop teaching all of a sudden?' Susan asked.

'Rob's offer of the cottage, partly. It came just before the summer term began and it happened there was someone who could fill the gap, so I didn't have much trouble giving notice. But I didn't tell Annette till I'd done it. I think perhaps she decided to marry me then to stop me doing anything still stupider. She agreed to come here . . .' He paused again and looked round. 'It's a grim little place really, isn't it, even without the thought of that poor child having been killed here? But I thought I could make it pleasant enough till we saw how things were going to work out. Now I don't know.'

Susan was looking at a framed photograph on the mantelpiece. 'Is that Annette?'

'Yes, only it isn't particularly like her,' Jocelyn said. 'She doesn't photograph well. For some reason a camera always turns her face into a mask. There's really much more life in it than that.'

'She looks beautiful, all the same.'

Susan would probably have said that whatever the face in the photograph had been like. To admire Annette, to yield everything to her in the way of beauty, charm, intelligence and goodness, was simple self-defence. Susan had come to understand that during the last few minutes. However, the statement happened to be true and had come out spontaneously. There was a Madonna quality about Annette. She had a calm, oval face, pale, shining hair that was parted in the middle and brushed smoothly back from her temples and eyes that, at least in the photograph, appeared curiously dark to go with such fair hair, and very gentle. It was easy to imagine young children adoring her, bringing flowers to school with them to lay on her desk and telling their somewhat sceptical yet jealous parents of her perfections.

Susan added, 'She reminds me of someone, I can't think who.'

'Perhaps you saw her here last summer,' Jocelyn suggested.

'I don't think so. I didn't even know she was here last summer.'

'She was, for a short time.'

'Was that when you met her?'

'Oh no, I've known her for years. We were even engaged for a time once, years ago. But it didn't work out then.' He took a long, thoughtful look at the photograph. There was an expression on his face that Susan did not understand, a sort of sadness and resignation. 'I never thought it would work out. That's why I never talked about her. I thought she was not for me. But I never stopped loving her, that was always the problem.'

'Yes, I see.'

'I *couldn't* talk about it, Susan.' There was a plea for forgiveness in his voice.

'Why should you?' She stood up. She went to the door of the kitchen. 'Surely there's something here we could be getting on with. All this crockery, can't we start washing it up? If it's only been unpacked this morning it can't have the murderer's fingerprints on it.'

Jocelyn came to look over her shoulder. The crockery was stacked on the table, the draining-board and the floor. Inappropriately, a bag of golf-clubs leant against a wall, tied into a bundle with some mops and brooms. Crumpled newspaper and fragments of straw were scattered everywhere.

'What a horrible mess,' he muttered.

'It looks an awful lot for just two people to use,' Susan said.

'Doesn't it?'

'I didn't know you played golf.'

'I don't, but Annette does. This stuff is mostly hers. The furniture too. She inherited it all from her mother who died some months ago. We'll have to do some weeding out to fit it in here, there's much too much. We might have done it at the other end, but the house was in Scotland and neither of us seemed to have the time to go there, so we just handed the keys over to the removal people and told them to bring everything. I'm beginning to regret it.'

'Well, where shall we get started? It ought to make it easier for the police if some of it's out of the way.'

'It ought, that's true. All right then, let's get down to it. The first thing is to boil a kettle. There's no hot water unless you light that awful contraption there.' He pointed at the ancient, rusted kitchen range.

Susan picked an electric kettle out of the litter, filled it at the dripping tap and plugged it into one of the most primitive looking electric plugs that she could remember seeing. But the kettle had hardly started to hum before the police arrived, not only Inspector Piggott and the sergeant who so obviously enjoyed the work of observing Susan, but a team of men with cameras and other apparatus, who indicated to her that she was distinctly in the way. Abandoning the idea of washing up, she told Jocelyn that she would return to do it next day, if she was allowed to, and left him.

Dawdling up the road, deep in thought, she was astonished to hear a voice shouting her name, then to see Conrad Ives running towards her with all the signs of being pursued by furies, of being desperate, scared and angry.

'Where the hell did you get to?' he bawled at her. 'Your sister's been mad with anxiety. So have I. So has everyone. You're never, never to do that again, do you understand? To vanish like that without saying anything!'

'How ridiculous!' Susan said. 'I only went to see Jocelyn. There was nothing whatever to worry about.'

'But how was anyone to know that? How was I to know where you were? One minute you were there, your sister said, and the next minute you were gone.'

'A regular Red Queen,' Susan said.

'Don't laugh. Anything might have happened. There's a killer loose, don't you realise? A maniac, probably, who's already killed one young girl. Anyway, that's the sort of thing one can't help thinking about at a time like this.'

With some astonishment, she began to take in the genuineness of his anxiety.

'I'm sorry, I really am,' she said. 'But still, you shouldn't have worried.'

'I'll go on worrying till this thing's cleared up, so for God's sake, don't do it again.' His voice grew calmer as they walked on together up the road. 'By the way, they still haven't found the python. And do you know why I think they haven't found it? I think it's because there never was one. I think the Riscoes made it up on purpose to get the police to search those woods.'

Susan stood still, staring at him. After a moment she said, 'I don't understand. Why should they want the woods searched?'

'Because they suspected something, of course.'

'Why do you have to be so silly. The python disappeared before Sandra was killed. There's absolutely no question of that. I saw her and talked to her myself the day after the alarm was sent out about the python.'

'Yes, but if the Riscoes saw something or found something before that . . .' His face was white and excited. 'I mean, if Sandra wasn't the only one . . .'

5

Susan shook her head. She knew that there was something wrong with the argument. She couldn't take it seriously. All the same, when Conrad had said goodbye to her at the Lasletts' door and had gone off on his motorbike, she found his idea a remarkably unpleasant one with which to be left alone.

At dinner Arthur looked thoughtful, very tired and was not to be drawn into discussion of the murder. After dinner he settled down to play Gilbert and Sullivan records to himself while Fiona vanished into the kitchen to cook a very elaborate cake, which was the sort of thing that she did nowadays if she wanted to take her mind off an unpleasant subject. Susan, in a mood to enjoy neither Gilbert and Sullivan nor the aromas of chocolate and vanilla, went upstairs.

The absurd thing about Conrad's idea, of course, the reason why she had known at once that it was only one of his fantasies, was that if Rob and Nina had found something suspicious in the woods where Rob prowled so often with the owl or the goshawk, they would simply have gone to the police and told them what they had found. Rob and Nina weren't likely to be afraid of the police. They weren't criminal, or even particularly devious people, who might be expected to invent a fantastic thing like the escape of an imaginary python rather than have a straightforward talk with a reasonable man like Inspector Piggott.

Or were they?

Lying restlessly awake in bed some hours later, with a square of starry sky showing through the open window, Susan again started brooding unhappily on how horribly easy it was to go wrong about people. Jocelyn's face haunted her, as it had looked when he had been talking about Annette. That expression had meant, hadn't it, that even now he wasn't sure that she loved him? That he loved her, of course, as he always had, even when he had come calling for Susan every few days, taking her about with him as he might have taken any affectionate pet creature, whose total acceptance of him had partly healed his hurt; but that even now, when Annette, for whatever reason, had married him, he was resigned to doing without much of her love.

Or could it possibly be the other way round?

Could that sad look have meant that Jocelyn had discovered that he himself was unable to love Annette any longer, was afraid that perhaps he had become unable to love anybody, because she had over-strained his power to love?

But Susan was half-asleep by the time that she thought of that. Remembering it in the morning, it seemed to be part of a dream. Confused and heavy-eyed, as if she had had too much to drink the night before, she went down very late to breakfast and heard from Fiona that Nina had just rung up to ask the three of them over for drinks before lunch.

Susan replied that she had promised Jocelyn to help him settle in.

'Oh, I expect he'll be going along too,' Fiona said. 'Rob's home, by the way, with the new falcon.'

She offered this piece of information with a gleam of amusement in her eyes, as if as a bait for Susan, though whether it was Rob who was supposed to be the bait, or the falcon, Susan did not know. It only made her marvel more than ever at the depth of misunderstanding at which nearly all human intercourse is conducted.

Immediately after breakfast she went to the cottage. Jocelyn was on a step-ladder in the sitting-room, continuing with the painting out of the cabbage roses. Two walls now had their first coat of white and a good deal of the third wall had been covered. Swishing his broad paintbrush backwards and forwards, he told Susan that the police had stayed for several hours the evening before, but that, so far as he knew, they had not discovered anything of importance. He told her also that just a little while before she had come round there had been a small invasion by the press, but that it appeared that from a journalist's point of view the discovery of a mere body in a wood, particularly since the victim had not been raped, was not very newsworthy.

'And I'd nothing much to tell them anyway,' Jocelyn said. 'After all, I never even saw the Taylors. Rob's been more helpful, however. He made some sketches of them both from memory, and I believe the one of the girl is being used on television to see if they can get an identification of her. From the doctor's report it seems definite that she was only fifteen or sixteen, so almost certainly she'd run away from home and tried to cover up all traces of who she was. The police think they know Taylor. From Fiona's description of him, together with that withered arm, they're pretty sure he's a man called Wall, who's been in and out of jail ever since he grew up.'

'For what sort of thing?' Susan had gone to the kitchen and filled the kettle, to heat some water for the washing-up that she and Jocelyn had abandoned the evening before.

'For most things,' he answered. 'Burglary, peddling dope, smuggling, living on women's immoral earnings. But he's a peaceable type in his way. He's got no record of violence.'

'Perhaps because of that withered arm.'

'I know. The reason he can't have killed the girl. All the same, the address he gave the removal people, a place in Islington, was a phoney. West's van with the furniture got there yesterday afternoon and found a small shoe shop, where he'd never been heard of.'

'What was the point of his doing a thing like that?'

Susan returned to the sitting-room door and looked up at Jocelyn on his step-ladder. He looked happy, painting, as irresponsibly cheerful as a young boy who has been allowed to show his skill in some normally prohibited adult craft.

'Well, it rather looks, at the least, as if he was running out on the girl, doesn't it?' he said. 'Suppose he told her he'd found a flat in London, made it look convincing by fixing up with West's to move the furniture, told her he was going on ahead to get

61

things ready at that end while she saw the stuff out here, and then took off into the blue.'

'Why couldn't he just go off into the blue without all the fuss and bother about the furniture?'

'I don't know. Perhaps it's the way his mind works.'

'It doesn't sound right to me,' she said. 'Over-elaborate. If I'd been him, I'd just have got into my car and driven away. She couldn't have done anything about it.'

'Unless there's something we don't know.'

'Such as?'

'Suppose for some reason he wanted to get a start before she realised she'd been run out on.'

'Because he'd taken something of hers?'

'Or because he meant to do something she could have prevented by giving him away to the police or somebody he meant to double-cross.'

'But all the same . . .' Susan was thinking of the glimpse that she had had of the girl dancing in this room after Taylor had gone, of her air of joy and excitement as she whirled round and round. 'She looked so glad to see him go,' she said. 'Glad about something, anyway, as if something was working out just as she wanted. I envied her, you know. I thought, I haven't been able to go crazy like that since I was a kid.'

Jocelyn gave her a quick smile. 'Not often, even then, I imagine. I should think you were a pretty solemn child.'

She grinned. 'Not as bad as you think. I seem to remember I was mostly rather cheerful.'

'Fiona's told me you always suffered from a rather serious view of life.'

'Fiona! Is anyone ever so wrong about one as one's own relations?' She turned back to the kitchen and the washing-up, raising her voice a little as she went on talking through the open door. 'Anyway, Fiona thinks it's a symptom of a mortal disease if you want to open a book.'

'So it is,' Jocelyn answered. 'It's the beginning of the end, the first stage along the road to the bifocals, the false teeth and the rubber tipped walking stick. Can you remember how old you were when you learnt to read, Susan?'

'Oh, I don't know – about five, I think.'

'So early? That means you must have contracted the habit even before the Riscoes, R. and N., started writing. You didn't cut your milk teeth on Porky Pye and Croc-the-Dile.'

'Goodness, no. I never could read them, anyway – only don't tell that to Rob and Nina.'

'I rather like them myself. It was an ingenious formula they hit on, that sort of compromise between Beatrix Potter and Damon Runyon.' He dipped his brush into the can of paint. 'You did like my play, didn't you? You haven't been saying to Rob and Nina, "I thought the thing was lousy, only don't tell poor Jocelyn, he'd be so terribly hurt." '

'No, I didn't.'

'I should be, you know – hurt to the quick.'

'No, but I didn't cut any teeth on it either,' Susan said. 'My second lot were ground in at school on people like Kipling and Newbolt. I loved them too, they were so beautifully easy to learn by heart. "Te-dum, te-dum, te-dum, te-dum, Te-dum, te-dum, te-dum . . ." But now it's perfectly maddening to have one's memory clogged with things like that and to find that there's less and less room for anything else.'

They both started laughing. They had slipped so easily into the tone of their old relationship that Susan had not even noticed it happening.

Because it was so comfortable, it did not interfere with their work. By twelve o'clock, when they left the cottage together to go to Bright's Farm, the china and glass had all been put away in the cupboards that Susan had scrubbed out and the first coat of paint in the sitting-room was complete and Jocelyn had begun work on the bathroom.

It was as they were walking along the lane to the farmhouse that Jocelyn suddenly remarked, 'Annette rang me up at the farm last night. She's arriving this afternoon.'

It was the first time that morning that he had mentioned Annette.

'Is she going to stay on?' Susan asked.

'Only for a day or two. The school term hasn't finished yet. But she's managed to get a few days off.' Jocelyn was silent for a moment. 'She hadn't heard about the murder and like a fool, I didn't tell her, so I'll have to do it when she gets here and she'll probably wish she hadn't come.'

'I'm sure she won't,' Susan said.

'Oh yes, she may.'

'But that sounds . . .'

'What?'

'Well . . .' What Susan had really wanted to tell him was that he had a bad habit of underrating his value to other people and through this could be far more unjust to them than he realised. But she had an uncomfortable feeling that he had been trying to lead her into saying something critical of Annette, so that the thing should be said without his being to blame for it. She said, 'Anyway, she'll have read all about the murder in this morning's papers, so if she turns up at all, you needn't worry.'

'Is there anything about it in the papers this morning?' he asked. 'I haven't seen them.'

'Neither have I, as a matter of fact.'

'As I was telling you, it's quite a little murder, as murders go. There wouldn't be more than a small paragraph about it, which Annette probably wouldn't see. No, I ought to have told her last night, but somehow I didn't.'

Just as somehow, Susan thought, he had failed to say certain other things to her at the time when they should have been said. And as somehow, no doubt, he always would. Never say anything unpleasant today if there was a chance that someone else would say it for you tomorrow. That was Jocelyn.

But Susan's knowledge that this was so did not help in the least to make her love him less. It only evoked a mood of tenderness, of wanting to shield this incompleteness of his from the harsher understanding of people who did not happen to love him.

When they reached the farmhouse he went immediately in search of the Sunday papers while Rob led Susan away to look at the peregrine falcon.

The bird was in a shed behind the studio, out of sight of the wooden block where Celia, the goshawk, was perched. Rob did not let Susan go into the shed, but only moved the cover of a small spyhole in the door so that she could look through. She could barely see the falcon in the darkness inside. A humped shape on one of the rafters, the outline of a predatory beak, were all that was visible.

'I put her in here to settle down in the dark after the journey,' Rob said. 'She was wild with fright and fury. Can you see her? She's a beauty, one of the finest I've ever seen.' His voice was warm with delight. 'Did I tell you we're going to call her Rosalind?'

'Yes, but not why you name all your creatures out of *As You Like It*,' Susan said. 'Because that's where even Adam, the python, comes from, isn't it? The name's got nothing to do with the old Adam.'

'Quite right,' Rob agreed. 'Actually it began in a more or less unintentional way with our first pet, a mongrel bitch who wandered in one day, liked the look of things and settled in. Someone asked us what breed she was and one of us said something about her being a poor thing but she seemed to think she was our own. So after that, of course, as we needed a name for her, we called her Audrey. Then we got the monkey, who's such a natural clown it seemed obvious to call him Touchstone. And since then we've simply stuck to the pattern. Jocelyn hates it. He calls it an atrocious impertinence to exploit Shakespeare for such a ridiculous purpose, with which I entirely agree.'

'When are you going to start waking Rosalind?'

By waking Susan meant the first step taken by many falconers in the training of a bird, the staying up with her all night, and sometimes, if the falconer has the strength for it, all the next day and the next night too, talking to her softly, stroking her plumage lightly with a feather, patiently offering food until at last, through sheer weariness and the novel discovery that there seems to be no harm in the man, the bird begins to trust him.

'I want to start tonight,' Rob said. 'I'll give Orlando his evening outing, then settle down with Rosalind in the studio. Actually, a lot of people don't believe in waking falcons as they do goshawks; they just hood them from the start till the bird gets used to them, but I don't much hold with that.'

'Staying up all night isn't my idea of fun,' Susan said.

'How do you know till you've tried it? Think of it, Susan—'

Rob's face lit up. 'To tame a creature as essentially wild and ferocious as a falcon – because they're real killers, remember – and all without a blow, or a curse, or even an angry look, because any one of those could ruin everything. And you do get angry, believe me. You get near to exploding with impatience and frustration. But all that you dare to use against the beast is enormous patience and cunning. You mustn't even look at her too steadily, because a straight stare, to her mind, is a threat. Yet in the end you win, not because she's frightened of you, or come to feel the slightest affection for you, but simply because she's recognised that it's a good idea to accept your offer of a partnership. A partnership of equals. And from the day that you let her fly free, without a creance, she can escape. She's no captive in a cage. If ever she wants to go, she can. And she won't be helpless in the wild either. She can hunt for herself, because you've taught her how. Even if she was taken from the nest, before her parents had taught her anything, as this one was, you'll have taught her how to be independent of you. Isn't that a tremendous challenge?'

Susan laughed. 'It's really she who holds you captive, isn't it, Rob?'

He covered the spyhole again. 'Aren't we all captives of something or other? And don't we like it? Take you, for instance. You'd a chance to escape, yet you didn't take it. You know, I'm very sorry you didn't. I think it was a mistake, my dear.'

'But can't I still go when I want to,' she said, 'like your falcon?'

'But haven't I just explained, in the end she won't want to? When I've finished with her, she'll always come back to me. I've only to show her the lure and give the whistle she'll recognise and down she'll come to my glove. Don't let that happen to you, Susan.'

'Why should it?'

'Because my nice quiet brother has a great deal of cunning – very gentle cunning – and a great deal of patience.'

Colour flared in Susan's cheeks. 'Why are you always so horrible about him, Rob? As if you hate him. Sometimes I think you do hate him.'

'Sometimes I do.'

'But why?'

'Because he always gets what he wants in the end. It's that patience of his.'

'But you've plenty of patience yourself. You've just explained how much you need to train a falcon.'

'I've only got it with dumb animals. With human beings I tend to get irritable rather quickly. Haven't you noticed that?'

'I've noticed you've a way of rushing in where most people fear to tread.'

'In other words, I'm talking about a lot of things that aren't my business. Only they are, they are.' He put a hand on her shoulder and turned her towards the studio. They walked slowly towards the door. 'Somebody's got to tell you you're in deadly danger, my child.'

'I don't think I am.'

'Of course you don't. But I saw your face when you came up the lane with Jocelyn. It was alight. You're far more beautiful when you're with him than you are at any other time, d'you know that? He does, of course. And he likes it too. But that doesn't mean that he doesn't love Annette. He does, he has for years. He's waited patiently and in the end he's got her. And being number three in a marriage of that sort isn't a life for anybody. None of which I'd trouble to say if I didn't see the possibility of a dreadful fidelity in you. You've the light of dedication in your eyes. Well, that's fine, but don't let it be to Jocelyn. He'll keep you hypnotised by his quite genuine need of you, while Annette patronises and exploits you.'

Susan stood still. 'Have you finished?'

'No,' he said, 'it's a theme I could develop for some time.'

'Well, your audience is fed up,' she said. 'It's all a lot of nonsense. If you're going on, I'm going looking for Nina.'

'Don't do that,' he said. 'She'll only talk about the murder and so will the others. Haven't you had enough of that? Come and talk to Celia. We mustn't let Rosalind put her nose out of joint.'

He led the way to where the goshawk sat preening herself on her block in the shade.

It was only then, as she followed him, that Susan realised that all the time that she and Rob had been talking, neither of them had said a word about the murder. She could think of no one but Rob with whom that would have been possible and with him it did not even seem odd.

'How will they like each other, the hawk and the falcon?' she asked, looking down at the goshawk, the bird with eyes so brilliantly golden that it has been called the Bird of the Sun.

'Rosalind probably won't mind Celia much,' Rob said, 'but if Celia ever gets loose, she'll dash Rosalind's brains out.'

'However long they've known each other?'

'However long.' He stooped and gently touched Celia's breast. She moved her head uneasily, so that she could keep one blazing yellow eye on Susan. 'Wouldn't you, you lovely thing? You'd dash out Susan's too, as soon as look at her, if she weren't a little big for you to take on. Which is lucky, because we don't want to lose her.'

They moved on to the big cage by the studio door, where Orlando, the owl, clopped his beak at them and hissed venomously.

Susan felt the unease she always did when she was close to him. 'He makes my blood run cold,' she said. 'But that's just what you like, isn't it, Rob? All that pent up ferocity in birds of prey. You love it.'

'Yes,' he answered. 'They don't compromise with you. They don't change their natures to suit you. And they're among the very few really savage creatures you can have in your home. There's fascination in that.'

'Is that why you wanted a python?' Susan asked. 'That's savage enough, isn't it?'

'No, as it happens, it isn't – not our Adam – he's a Rock Python, the lighter coloured kind that snake-charmers use because they're so easily tamed. He's a very friendly, amiable creature. All the same, he was one of my mistakes. Nina can't stand him. So I've promised to get rid of him if we ever see him again.'

'Do you think you will?'

Susan had turned from the owl's cage and was looking into the studio. Suddenly it occurred to her that there was no gap in the row of drawings. Where Nina had torn one down a head of

Sandra, the dead girl, had been pinned up. But as she looked at this, Susan found her memory jolted into visualising distinctly the drawing that had been there before, a Madonna-like head with serene eyes and forehead, with hair parted in the middle and brushed back from the temples. It had always haunted her vaguely as having a subtlety usually beyond Rob's reach except at times in his drawings of birds. Susan knew now, of course, why Jocelyn's photograph of Annette had seemed familiar.

'I doubt it,' Rob was saying. He did not sound much concerned. He was standing behind Susan and when she glanced round at him, she saw that he too was looking across the studio at the picture of Sandra, to whom he had given a softly rounded, stupid, blankly innocent face, but there was a blindness in his gaze as if he were not really looking at the picture. His bright eyes were intent, but on something much farther off than the picture.

What was he seeing? Sandra, as she must have looked when they found her in the wood; as Susan, thank God, had not had to see her? No, she thought, and all of a sudden had one of her curious moods of feeling afraid of Rob. No, he's seeing the picture of Annette. He knows that Nina tore it up. He knows she's in love with Jocelyn and can't bear his having married Annette. And that's the real reason why Rob hates Jocelyn so.

Yet he had let Jocelyn have the cottage. He had brought Jocelyn here to his very gates, where Nina could see him every day. Why? What had made him do it?

As if this hatred of Jocelyn were a threat to herself as well as to him, Susan became tense with apprehension. She had to get away from Rob.

'Let's go and find the others,' she said abruptly and started to walk away.

Rob followed her slowly.

As they joined the others in the sitting-room of the farmhouse, Fiona, who was just reaching for her usual gin-and-tonic from the tray that Jocelyn was carrying round, looked from Susan to Rob and said dryly, 'Been showing Susan the livestock, Rob?'

He nodded without speaking, turning to watch Nina, who was trying to persuade Touchie, the monkey, to come down from the top of a tall bookcase, where he was gleefully playing with a necklace of gold chains that Fiona had been wearing that morning.

'You blasted creature, come down!' Nina yelled shrilly at the monkey. 'Come down or I'll murder you, I really will, you horrible imp, you beastly midget! You don't know what I'll do to you when I get hold of you! Rob – Rob, you can reach him, can't you? Do get him down. He's snatched Fiona's necklace.'

'Don't worry,' Fiona said. 'Leave him in peace. We'll get it presently.'

Jocelyn brought Susan a drink. She took it and sat down on the hearthrug beside Oliver, the old pointer, who laid a heavy head on her knee and gazed up at her with sentimental affection.

'Rob, we've just been talking about the Taylors,' Arthur said. 'There's something I'm curious about. How long ago did they give you notice they were going to quit the cottage?'

'They didn't,' Rob said. 'I gave them notice.'

'Wasn't that rather difficult? It's usually very difficult to get rid of a sitting tenant from low-priced property. The law's with them all the way and to hell with the landlord.'

'It isn't so difficult with people like the Taylors.' Rob stepped on to a chair, caught Touchie and disentangled the necklace from his avid little paws, while Touchie chattered at him malignantly, then leapt to his usual perch on Nina's shoulder. 'Here you are, Fiona.'

'Thanks, Rob.' Fiona fastened the necklace round her neck. 'Perhaps the Taylors wanted to go,' she suggested. 'Was that it? I mean, perhaps they'd simply have flitted, if you hadn't happened to give them notice first.'

'I don't know, but I know I'd only to hint that the police might be about to take an interest in them for them to be eager to get the matter settled very expeditiously,' he said.

'And were the police actually taking an interest in them?' Arthur asked curiously.

'Not that I know of, but I was,' Rob said.

'And you mean to say you'd only to suggest—?'

Arthur's question was never finished for at that moment the

glass of the window was shattered by a half-brick that thudded heavily into the room, sending splinters of glass flying in all directions.

6

Arthur moved first. He threw open the broken window, jumped out into the middle of a flowerbed and raced off across the lawn. He was out of sight round the corner of the house by the time that Rob had stepped down from the chair on which he had been standing when the brick flew into the room, or Jocelyn put down the drink that he had been holding.

Afterwards Susan reflected how unexpected this had been. That her somewhat stiff and cautious brother-in-law should have had quicker reactions, as well as far more presence of mind, than anyone else there, did not fit her picture of him at all.

When they all streamed out into the garden, led by the furiously barking Oliver, Arthur already had hold of the collar of a short, struggling figure and was wresting a second half-brick out of his hand.

'Call him off, somebody!' the intruder shouted. 'Stop him, can't you? I haven't done anything.'

Rob shouted at the dog and Fiona shouted at Arthur, 'It's Conrad Ives, Arthur – let him go!'

Breathing hard, Arthur let go of his captive, but he kept hold of the half-brick.

'He was going to heave this at the window, I swear he was,' he said. He straightened his own collar and tie and smoothed his hair. 'Weren't you?' he asked Conrad with a rasp of parade ground severity.

'I was not,' said Conrad through clenched teeth. His sandy hair was on end and his eyes were wild. 'I'd just taken it from some kids who were going to send it after the other one. That was no reason to assault me.'

'What kids?' Arthur asked. 'I didn't see any.'

'I'd just scared them off.'

'I didn't see them,' Arthur reiterated.

'Who were they, Conrad?' Nina asked. 'Village children? Children we know? And why should they do a thing like that?'

'Because of the python.'

'The *python*?' she said incredulously.

'Suppose you come in, Conrad,' Rob suggested, 'and have a drink and tell us what it's all about.'

'Thank you, Mr Riscoe, but I don't want to take up your time,' Conrad answered aloofly. 'I only came to inquire—'

'*Oh, come in, Conrad!*' Susan had a special tone of voice for Conrad, in which there was a ferocity hardly ever evoked in her by anyone else. 'Come in and tell us your wonderful story, whatever it is.'

'I haven't got a wonderful story,' he snarled back at her. 'I came to ask Mr Riscoe if the python had been found yet, that's all, that's absolutely all. Then I saw these kids . . . Well, all right, thanks, Mr Riscoe, I'll come in if I may.'

'And I apologise,' Arthur said. 'I was over-hasty. I'm sorry.'

'No hard feelings,' Conrad muttered in a tone markedly lacking in sincerity.

They all returned to the sitting-room.

As they found their drinks again and Rob poured one out for Conrad, Jocelyn fetched a dustpan and brush from the kitchen and began sweeping up the fragments of glass which had been scattered all over the room.

'Oh, leave it, leave it!' Nina cried in exasperation. 'You're too damned domesticated these days. What's a little broken glass?'

'Not nice for a dog to walk about on,' Rob remarked. 'Thanks, Jocelyn.'

'I want to hear about these children who come and throw bricks at us,' she said. 'Who were they, Conrad?'

Jocelyn had gone on crawling about the floor, sweeping up the splinters. He observed softly to Susan, who was back on the hearthrug and on a level with him, 'Dramatic stuff, broken glass. It shivers into such an unreasonable number of bits and they seem to get everywhere. I remember I was in a room once when

73

someone drove a golf ball through the window. It felt almost like being shot at . . .' He dropped his voice. 'Who is he, Susan?'

'Conrad? A reporter from the *Swelsden Weekly Advertiser*,' she whispered back.

'Friend of yours?'

'Yes and no.'

A muscle in Conrad's cheek began to twitch. He was replying to Nina, but had obviously overheard what Susan had said.

'I don't know the actual children, Mrs Riscoe,' he was saying, 'but I've seen them around the village. I think they come from one of those cottages opposite the Dragon, the one with the pear tree against the wall.'

'The Merrows' cottage?' Nina asked. She clawed at her shaggy brown hair, so that it looked as if she had been out in a gale. 'But the Merrows are nice people.'

'There were three of them,' Conrad said. 'Two boys and a girl.'

'All very fair and plump, with rosy cheeks?'

'That sounds like them,' he agreed. 'But they ran off as soon as they saw my motor bike. I couldn't identify them for certain.'

'But they're nice,' Nina said in growing distress. 'We know them all quite well. Mrs Merrow sometimes comes and gives me help in the house.'

'Well, the trouble now is that a rumour's gone round the place that Sandra Taylor was strangled by your python, and naturally you're held responsible,' Conrad explained.

'Sandra strangled by the python?' Nina's voice rose shrilly. 'You aren't serious!'

'I'm sorry, I am,' he said. 'I've heard it myself.'

She turned to Rob. 'It's completely impossible, isn't it? It couldn't have happened.'

He looked more intrigued than worried.

'I don't honestly know what Adam might be capable of if he was scared,' he said. 'In general I believe people greatly exaggerate the sort of thing that kind of snake can do, just as there are fantastic stories about the size a python or an anaconda can grow to – forty feet and more. Actually thirty feet is quite a respectable size even for *Python Reticulatas*, which is a much larger snake

74

than Adam. A Rock Python isn't likely to grow much beyond fifteen or sixteen feet—'

'But *could* he have strangled that girl?' Nina cried frantically. 'That's what I'm asking – is it *possible*?'

'Since the police say she was strangled by a pair of hands – no,' Rob said. 'A snake hasn't got hands.'

'Could they be wrong?'

'About a good many things, yes, but about that, I shouldn't think so.'

'Look, Mrs Riscoe,' Conrad said, 'I didn't mean to give you the idea there are any sensible people around who believe the story. I'm sorry if I did. It's just one of those legends that start up in a place like this, like – well, that it's those things they shoot up into space that keep upsetting the weather – you know the sort of thing. I shouldn't worry about it if I were you. It'll die down of itself.'

'But the Merrow children . . . if *they'll* do a thing like that, what's going to happen next?'

'Nothing,' Rob said. 'Some other rumour's bound to start soon, which will switch their attention to somebody else.'

'If I were you, Nina,' Jocelyn said, brushing up glass splinters around her feet, 'I'd drop in on the Merrows and say a quiet word to them. If they're nice people, as you say, and you're normally on good terms with them, you ought to be able to sort things out quite easily.'

'Only what's the good of a quiet word with anybody when we've got the press in our midst?' she asked. 'Conrad, you came here for a story about the python and you seem to have got one. "Villagers Stone Owners of Dangerous Reptile." How's that for a headline? Will you print it?'

He smiled as he finished his drink. 'Reporters don't write their own headlines, you know. And children throwing stones at windows aren't really news, are they? It goes on all the time. But if you ever find the python and I could have a picture of it, with you, Mrs Riscoe, stroking it or something, with a brief description of its probable adventures – well, that's the sort of thing the readers of the *Advertiser* would really enjoy. Thanks for the drink. Goodbye.'

He went out without even glancing in Susan's direction, which possibly was sensible of him since she at least could recognise the tone of voice he used when he did not mean a single word that he was saying.

Arthur, who had been listening with a singularly expressionless face, stood up and went to the broken window. Looking out, he said, 'He's up to something, isn't he? I wonder if there really were any children.'

'Oh, Arthur, please, don't you get fanciful now!' Fiona said. 'We don't want another libellous rumour going the rounds.'

'Well, I got outside pretty quickly and I didn't see any children,' he said. 'I just saw Ives standing there with the brick in his hand.'

'Because you were too excited,' she said. 'You aren't accustomed to jumping out of windows.'

'All the same, that boy's up to something,' he insisted. 'Don't you think so, Rob?'

Rob shrugged his shoulders. 'I don't imagine it matters, even if he is.'

But that did not satisfy Arthur. At the time he said no more, but presently, as he and Fiona and Susan were walking home, he said explosively, 'Honestly, Fiona, I didn't see any children. I swear that boy was going to throw that brick.'

'But why should he?' she asked.

'I don't know. Has he some private grudge against the Riscoes, perhaps?'

'Ask Susan,' Fiona said. 'She's the one who knows him.'

'Do you, Susan?' Arthur asked. 'Do you know him well?'

'Moderately,' she answered.

'Well, what do you think about him? What's he like?'

'He's in love with Susan, for one thing,' Fiona said.

Susan flared up. 'Can't you ever think of anything else? He isn't in love with me, he's just – oh, I suppose attracted. He isn't in love with anything except his silly idea of becoming a journalist.'

'What's silly about that?' Arthur asked.

'I don't mean it's silly in itself, it's just silly of him to have it.'

'Why?'

76

'Because, if he was any good, he wouldn't have got stuck all this time on the *Swelsden Weekly Advertiser*, would he? And he's really quite intelligent, so he could do better at something else if he'd try.'

'But you think he lacks ambition.'

'I think he's bone lazy.'

Arthur laughed. 'That isn't how he struck me. For the last day or two he's been under my feet wherever I've turned and that must have required quite an expenditure of energy.'

'He's only rushing round in circles. It won't get him anywhere.'

Arthur turned to Fiona. 'You know, I never realised Susan put such a value on worldly success. I thought the young in general were rather against it.'

'I don't put a value on success,' Susan said indignantly, 'but I like a person to use his brains, if he happens to have any. Conrad got that job in the first place because his mother's related to the proprietor of the *Advertiser* and he only stays on because he knows they won't fire him however little he bothers.'

'I doubt that, somehow,' Arthur said. 'An employer will stand only so much, even from his own relations. So perhaps Conrad has virtues you haven't observed. Are his family local people?'

'Yes, didn't you know? They were farmers. They owned Bright's Farm for generations. I think at some stage a Bright daughter married an Ives and Conrad's their great-great-grandson, or something like that.'

'*Is* he now – that's interesting,' Arthur said thoughtfully. 'Couldn't it back up this feeling of mine, perhaps, that he did throw that brick at the window? A sudden temptation to get even, you know, that he couldn't resist. A momentary insanity.'

'Well, he has lots of moments of momentary insanity,' Susan said.

'Why did his family give the place up? Did they go broke?'

'Lord, no, they've pots of money. But his father was killed in an accident and his mother married again, and her second husband owns a lot of hotels dotted about the country and he's fearfully rich, and Conrad never wanted to be a farmer anyhow, so his mother sold up here and they all went to live in London. And

Conrad went to St Paul's and of course he could have gone on to Oxford, or anywhere else he liked, but instead he chose to come back here to work on that frightful little paper.'

Fiona said, 'D'you know, this is all news to me? Perhaps you're right, Arthur; perhaps he did throw that brick, because he couldn't stand the sight of other people living in his old home. But tell me something, why were you interested in how long ago the Taylors gave notice? You were just asking Rob about it when the brick crashed into the room. Do you think it's important, for some reason?'

'Oh, I was just puzzled because it happened so secretly,' he said. 'We see the Riscoes fairly frequently, yet they never said anything to us about the Taylors moving away, or Jocelyn and his wife coming to live here.'

'Are you annoyed with Nina and Rob because they didn't tell us anything about Jocelyn's marriage?' she asked. 'I'm a bit annoyed myself. It wasn't particularly friendly of them. Still, I suppose it's their own business.'

'Strictly their own,' he replied. 'No, I was merely curious about what pressure Rob really brought to bear on Taylor to make him leave. But we shan't find out. Rob's a very secretive creature. What are we having for lunch?'

'The rest of that cold chicken and salad. You know, you could probably find out anything you want to know from Nina.'

'She may not know much. I'd be very surprised if she knows half as much about Rob as she thinks she does.'

They both laughed.

It made Susan's irritability increase sharply. For the last hour she had been sliding deeper and deeper into a mood of hating everybody. That included even Jocelyn. Everything seemed stupid and dreary and depressing and she wished that she were back in her bed-sitting-room in London.

Yet she had enjoyed the morning working in the cottage with Jocelyn, had enjoyed it as much as anything that had happened for a long time. She had felt no jealousy of Annette, had not minded the fact that the work was in a sense being done for her. There had even been a kind of contentment in the thought. Susan's only anxiety then had been for Annette to take a liking

78

to her and neither distrust her nor despise her. If she did either of those things it would be intolerable. But why should she? Why shouldn't Annette like her? A peace of mind that Susan did not feel very often had settled upon her and made the morning astonishingly happy.

She knew quite well when the happiness had ended. It had been during that talk with Rob, when he had warned her against Jocelyn and against becoming a number three in his marriage. For, to be quite honest with herself, somewhere at the back of her mind some such hope had formed. If she asked very little for herself, she had started to think, and if Annette liked her, might she not be spared the desolation of giving up Jocelyn entirely? But Rob had knocked that on the head very effectively, even more effectively than he knew, for although what he had meant to do was to make the situation sound dangerous, what he had actually succeeded in doing was to make it sound exceedingly childish, and that was a far graver matter to Susan.

'Bloody old father fixation, and so on, and so on, and so on,' she muttered bitterly to herself as she went up to her bedroom after lunch and settled down to work her way through another slab of Brachet.

But first she took a look at the cottage from her window. In the room where she had seen Sandra dancing she could see Jocelyn putting on the second coat of white paint. It looked as if Annette had not arrived yet.

Later in the afternoon Inspector Piggott called on the Lasletts again. He wanted to ask Fiona and Susan if they had observed how many suitcases Taylor had put into his car. Fiona shook her head and said that she hadn't given the matter a thought. Susan considered the question carefully and said, 'I think there were two suitcases.'

'And do you remember if he brought them out of the house one at a time or together?' Inspector Piggott asked.

'I think he had them out in the road already when I looked out of the window,' she said. 'But he must have brought them out one at a time, mustn't he? He's got that withered arm.'

'I was hoping for some check on how much strength he has in it,' the inspector explained. 'If you'd seen him carrying both cases at the same time, for instance, it would have told us something.'

'You haven't found him yet?'

'No,' he said. 'But we've found out he was seen in London on Friday evening by one of his old friends. An old friend who's quite useful to the police occasionally. So it shouldn't take us long to run him to earth.'

'And the men from West's,' Fiona said, 'have you found out anything special about them?'

'They've been questioned, naturally.' His gaze slid away from Fiona's to the refuge of the incomprehensible painting above the fireplace. 'Their accounts of themselves appear to be perfectly satisfactory.'

'Which,' Fiona said to Susan as soon as he had left, 'I'll bet you anything you like they weren't. Did you notice how he couldn't look me in the eye when he said it?'

'I thought he was just telling you in a polite sort of way to mind your own business,' Susan said.

'Well, if all this isn't my business, I'd like to know what is. Oh, God, this horrible day! I wish it would end.'

Fiona returned to the kitchen and whiled away the rest of the afternoon by making an extremely elaborate chocolate mousse, which required eight eggs and a lot of brandy and had to be kept in the refrigerator for three days before being eaten.

That it did need to be kept was fortunate, for none of them had any appetite that evening. They sat over their drinks for longer and drank more than usual, then agreed that bread and cheese was all that they could face. Susan did not even want the bread and cheese. The drink had made her head feel hot and heavy and she found herself wanting to cry, not for any particular reason but simply because life had started to appear so sad and so silly. To keep at bay the extremely silly tears, she escaped from Arthur and Fiona as soon as she could, fetched a jersey from her room and started out into the dusk to see if a short walk would work off the effects of gin and depression.

At the gate she came face to face with a woman who barred her way.

Susan had never seen her before. The woman wore a loose coat

80

and a headscarf that completely hid her hair. Thick make-up almost hid, though not entirely, the ravages of tears on her sharp, triangular face. She thrust out a hand and grasped the sleeve of Susan's jersey with thin, strong fingers in a black fabric glove from which Susan recoiled as she would have from the fierce talons of a falcon.

'I'm her mother,' the woman said. 'Sandra's mother. You aren't going out, are you? I've got to speak to you.'

7

'It must be my sister you want,' Susan said. 'Mrs Laslett.'

'Is that her name? The lady who lives here. Don't you live here?' The woman still had hold of Susan's arm.

'No, I'm only on a visit. It must be my sister you want.'

'Didn't you know my Sandra?'

'I spoke to her just once.'

'And Stan Wall – Taylor – did you know him?'

Susan shook her head. She wanted to disengage her arm, because the woman's touch gave her a feeling of physical repulsion, but the woman seemed to feel that if she let Susan go, she would lose her.

Moving still closer, she stared at Susan with red-veined dark eyes which looked both eager and frightened. Their red and swollen lids were patchily covered with green eye-shadow, so that it looked as if they had been bruised in a fight.

'I've got to talk to someone,' she said. 'I can't sit there in the hotel all by myself, I can't stand it. And I've been to the cottage where they say she lived, but there's nobody there just now, it's all shut up and quiet.'

'Come in and see my sister then,' Susan said. 'She knew Sandra better than I did.'

The woman looked dubiously up at the house. 'She did? Yes, it's like Sandra said, big and modern and everything. Only she said she lived here herself, you know, she didn't say anything about any Mrs Laslett.'

'Sandra told you she lived in this house?'

'A house like this, anyway. Poor kid, day-dreaming as usual. I ought to have known.'

'Then,' Susan said thoughtfully, 'you knew she was here all along. You knew she was here with Taylor.'

'I did not!' The thin face twitched and darkened with anger. 'She sent me a card, a letter-card, that's all, saying she was all right and not to worry and how she was living in this nice big house. I showed it to the police back home. Much use they were. I haven't known where she was, or Stan either, for more than a year. I've been crazy over it all, I've lost weight, had dizzy spells ... What d'you mean, I knew she was here? She was only fifteen!'

'I'm sorry,' Susan said. 'I'm very sorry. Do come in now and meet my sister and brother-in-law. They'll tell you everything they can, though I don't think it'll be very much. But you'd like some tea or coffee, I expect. Have you had anything to eat this evening?'

With a sigh, the woman let go of Susan's arm. 'Thanks, I had a sandwich. I'm all right, I don't want to trouble anyone.'

'Well, do come in.'

'I don't want to trouble anyone.'

The woman's manner had subtly changed since she had first barred Susan's way, and now it was as if the thought of going into the house actually intimidated her. When Susan opened the door and motioned to her to go in ahead of her, she moved forward with awkward steps, folding her hands together primly on the handle of her handbag, respectability enveloping her like a shroud.

Susan took her into the sitting-room where Fiona and Arthur were sitting hand in hand on the long black sofa, watching television. To the mother of the murdered girl they must have appeared almost heartlessly serene. Susan started to tell them who the woman was, then realised that she did not know her name and turned to her questioningly.

'My name's Mrs Collis,' the woman said. 'Maureen Collis.'

'Sandra's mother,' Susan explained. 'She'd like to talk to you.'

Arthur and Fiona both got quickly to their feet and Arthur switched off the television.

As the light in the screen died away the room all at once became strangely bleak and lifeless, dim with the beginning of twilight. Arthur moved about rapidly, turning on several lights, as if to distract attention from some feeling roused in him by Mrs Collis. Fiona, on the other hand, stood quite still, unusually slow to remember to become a hostess. It struck Susan as extraordinarily interesting to see how deeply the two of them really resented the intrusion of tragedy into their pleasant lives.

But in a moment they had adjusted themselves. They shook Mrs Collis's hand. Arthur took her coat, offered her a drink, a cigarette and his sympathy, then drew the curtains briskly, shutting out the eeriness of the dusky woods in which Sandra's body had been found. Fiona went out to make coffee and sandwiches.

Mrs Collis refused the drink but reached avidly for the cigarette.

Without coat and headscarf, she looked quite different from Susan's first impression of her. She was an extremely thin woman, with the boniness of under-nourishment and bad nerves. Her dark hair had been flattened to her head by the scarf and was wispy and lifeless. She wore a suit of black and white rayon which either dated back to a time when she had been far plumper, or else had been handed on to her by someone else. She looked drained and exhausted, yet full of that frenzied, desperate energy that keeps some people going till they drop.

'It feels queer, being in here,' she said, looking round her, coughing hoarsely over the smoke and hitting herself punitively on the chest to stop it. 'It's all just as Sandra described it. I was just telling this young lady, Mr Laslett, I had a card from Sandra, no address or anything and the postmark London, saying she and Stan were living in a lovely modern house like this. I half-believed her too, because Stan always said he'd make a lot of money some day, and now and then he really did, though he never learnt how to keep any of it, so he never got anywhere that I know of. Of course, Sandra wrote like that because she was ashamed of what she'd done to me, going off like that and taking Stan. I showed the card to the police. I said, "Surely to God now you can find her. She describes the place she's living in and all." But they said there were thousands of places like that all over the country, even if what she wrote was true, which, they said, it probably wasn't.'

84

'You know Taylor then?'

Arthur had remained standing and was looking down at her with something so deliberate in his air of kindness that Susan felt certain that, like herself, he was having to control a physical repulsion roused in him by Mrs Collis.

'Not Taylor – Stan Wall,' she corrected him. 'Yes, he and I – well, we were supposed to be getting married some time. Not that I ever thought we really should. I always knew what sort he was and that it wouldn't last. But I never thought of his going off with Sandra, never. A child like that. And now to do what he's done . . .'

She choked and tears began to spill out of her eyes, but it was clear that now that she had started to talk, nothing could stop her.

'Why did he have to go and do a thing like that, will anybody tell me?' she said. 'He could have sent her home when he was through with her, he could have sent me a line to say where she was, so I could have come and got her. But to do what he did . . . I'd never have thought it, even of Stan. I knew he was up to most things, but he always said, and I always believed, he didn't hold with violence. "It's not worth it," he said, "it's a mug's game," he said. Besides him not being built for it, with that arm of his, and it's the truth I never saw him violent. He could be very ill-natured, he could say things you thought you'd never live to forgive, but I never saw him lift his hand against anybody. But Sandra was just a kid and she wouldn't have been expecting trouble, that's how it must have been. He took her by surprise somehow. He wouldn't have been scared of what she'd do back. He'd know he could do what he liked with her.'

'Mrs Collis,' Arthur said quickly, as she drew breath, 'haven't the police told you they don't believe it was Wall who killed your daughter? They don't believe it could have been done in the way it was by a man with one withered arm.'

'He did it,' she said. 'However he worked it, he did it, it was Stan. It stands to reason. He was tired of her, but she knew all about him, so he couldn't be rid of her till she wanted. That's what I told the police. He's cunning, I said, and he's made it look like he couldn't have done it on account of his arm, but that's

85

what he's like, I said, he's ever so crafty. If he wanted to kill you he wouldn't do it all of a sudden in anger, he'd sit down quietly and think it all out first, just so you'd say a man like him couldn't have done it. That's what he's always been like.'

'I see. Then do you think he may have had an accomplice who did the murder for him?'

'He might've. Or he might've thought of some clever way of doing it all by himself. If you ask me, that's what it was. He wasn't one to trust other people if he could help it.'

'Do you know anything about his friends?'

'Friends!' she said harshly. 'What friends does a man like that have? Look how he treated me. Is that the way to keep friends?'

'Perhaps I used the wrong word,' Arthur said. 'I should have said colleagues. People in the same line of business.'

She shrugged the thin shoulders inside the floppy jacket. 'However he worked it, it was Stan,' she said.

She had smoked her cigarette down to the last half-inch and was still holding it tightly between stained fingers. As Arthur offered her another she sucked once more at the stub, then lit the second cigarette from it, ignoring the flame of Arthur's lighter. When Fiona came in with a plate of sandwiches and some hastily made coffee, Mrs Collis reached hungrily for a sandwich, but kept her cigarette going and in a moment had forgotten the sandwich, leaving it on her plate with only one bite taken out of it.

'I've told the police all about Stan,' she said. 'I've told them everything I know, which is something I used to think I'd never do. Even when he went off with Sandra, I didn't tell them half, I only said my daughter's gone off with Mr Wall, the lodger. I'm a widow, I said, and got this kid to bring up and no one to help me, so I've always had a lodger to help make ends meet. My daughter isn't bringing any money in yet, I said, she's too young, she's still at school and that's where she's going to stay too and get a good education, not like me . . .' A convulsion of coughing stopped her.

'How did you hear what had happened?' Arthur asked. 'How did you know where to come?'

'A neighbour told me,' Mrs Collis said. 'She saw it on TV. She

86

said, "They had a picture of your Sandra on TV," she said, "I'm sure it was Sandra, and they said anyone who could identify her was to get in touch with the police." So I got in touch with them. I thought, they'll be fed up, I'm always getting in touch with them, they'll say this girl wasn't anything like Sandra. I don't know what I was hoping, that they'd say that or they wouldn't. But they didn't. They sent a car straight round for me and showed me the picture and it was Sandra all right.'

'Where were you?' Arthur asked. 'Had you far to come to get here?'

'Only from Birmingham.'

'Are you staying in Swelsden for the night?'

'For several nights. They said I've got to stay till after the inquest. They've treated me all right. They've got me a room at the Royal and it's nice enough. But I couldn't stay there by myself tonight. I wanted to go out and see where she lived and all. I wasn't thinking of coming to see you, I didn't mean to trouble anyone, but the cottage was all shut up and nobody there and then I saw her coming out of here—' She nodded towards Susan. 'So all of a sudden I made up my mind to speak to her.'

'You must be very tired,' Arthur said. 'When you're ready to go, I'll drive you back to your hotel.'

It sounded kind. It even was kind, in a way, although, as Susan recognised, it was also a manœuvre for encouraging Mrs Collis to leave. Arthur was afraid that if something of the sort were not done she might stay for ever. Anyone as tightly wound up as this woman was would not be able to stop herself talking on and on, saying the same things over and over again, until some fairly drastic measures were taken by somebody else.

But she did not want help. 'I'm all right, thank you, Mr Laslett,' she said. 'I wouldn't dream of troubling you. I can get the bus at the corner. It goes right past the hotel.'

'It wouldn't be any trouble,' Arthur said. 'Do let me take you.'

'No, thank you, I'm all right,' she repeated.

Fiona looked at her watch. 'You'd have almost half an hour to wait for the next bus, Mrs Collis. If you won't let my husband drive you in, have some more coffee. Have another sandwich.'

'No, thank you,' Mrs Collis said, but accepted a cigarette, lighting it in the same way as she had the last.

'I was meaning to go back to the cottage and see if the people have got home,' she said. 'I don't want to bother them, it's just a feeling I've got that I want to see the place Sandra lived in. I'd like to understand why she left home. It wasn't just Stan, that's what I think. He wasn't so special and she'd got looks, she knew she had, she could take her pick, she knew that too. If it was just a man she wanted, she could have done a lot better than him.'

She stood up and moved towards the door. She did it suddenly and yet there was a vagueness about it, an air of drifting, as if she were hardly aware of what she was doing. Without looking at anyone in the room, she went on talking. Susan thought that she would still be talking when she was out in the road with no one to hear her. In the lonely months since Sandra and Stan Wall had gone, Mrs Collis must have learnt to people the shadowy world through which she blundered her blind unhappy way with imaginary listeners who were always there and always patient.

'What I think,' she was saying, 'is she wanted to get away from me and her home, and Stan was just there and willing enough. She'd a fearful strong will of her own and not much sense. She couldn't stand it if anyone corrected her. Not that I ever did as much as I ought, I never had the heart to, her being all I had. It's hard for a woman bringing up a child by herself when she's got to go out to work. But I did all I could, honest to God I did, I gave her everything I could manage. But it didn't suit her, she wanted to get away . . .'

When she had gone Arthur fell on the sandwiches that their visitor had not touched as if he had not eaten all day.

'Susan!' he exclaimed in a fiercer tone than she had ever heard him use. 'Susan, my child, if you find any more strange women wandering about the garden, or strange men, don't bring them in! Do you understand me? Don't – whatever else you do – *don't* bring them in!'

'Darling, Susan couldn't help it,' Fiona said. 'You'd have done it yourself. You couldn't have helped feeling sorry for her.'

'Sorry for her? Of course, I'd have felt, I do feel, sorry for her! And is there any feeling that leaves you feeling quite so wrung out as that kind of feeling sorry? I'm tired, I've had a hell of a day, we've all had a hell of a day, and tomorrow I've got to do a normal job of work . . . Sorry, Susan.' He had been roaming wildly round the room as if getting ready to smash the place up, but now he managed to stand still and smile at her. 'Don't take any notice of me. Of course you had to bring her in.'

'I wish she'd let you drive her into Swelsden,' Fiona said. 'I don't like the thought of her wandering about out there by herself. It'll soon be quite dark.'

He sighed. 'All right, I'll go after her and see she gets safely on the bus.'

'I didn't mean . . .'

'All right, all right, I'm going.' He reached for another sandwich and went out.

But in only a minute or two he came in again and now was smiling.

'She's found other company already,' he said. 'Young Ives. I didn't interfere. Bless the poor woman, she's probably doing us a good turn; heading him off, I mean, when he was coming here. Now you aren't going to say I've got to feel sorry for Ives because he hasn't got his story about the python, or because he feels dispossessed by the Riscoes, or anything else, are you? You aren't going to say I've got to sit and listen to him if he does walk in? Because if you are, you're going to be disappointed. I'm going to bed and I'm not going to listen to anybody till tomorrow morning.'

'All right, you poor old thing,' Fiona said. 'Go off to bed. I'll come too, I think. I'm very tired.'

But when Arthur had gone out she stayed on in the sitting-room. She looked at Susan with an uncertain frown. 'Do you think Conrad's coming here?' she asked.

'How should I know?'

Susan's own tiredness had hit her all of a sudden like a weight that was being pressed inexorably down on her brain. The last thing she wanted was to see Conrad that evening.

'Don't worry,' she added. 'If he does come, I won't let him in.'

'I was just going to say,' Fiona said, 'he might like to finish these sandwiches and you could make some more coffee.'

Susan shook her head. 'I'm going to bed too.'

'But if he starts ringing the bell . . .'

'Oh, all right, I'll answer it. I won't let him disturb you.'

'He'll know we're all in, you see, and he probably wouldn't think we'd go to bed so early, so he might think we were being unpleasant on purpose, and I shouldn't like that.'

'His skin isn't as thin as all that, you needn't worry. Anyway, I should think he'll stick as close as he can to Sandra's mother all the evening – if he has any of the makings of a newspaperman. Which I doubt.'

'I know you do. But he is in love with you, you know, Susan.' Fiona paused in the doorway to look curiously at her sister. 'Doesn't that mean anything to you?'

'Not much.'

'I thought today he'd an odd sort of charm. Quite a lot of charm really. Well, good-night.'

She went upstairs.

Susan, left alone in the sitting-room with the thought that Fiona's discovery of Conrad's charm had followed somewhat hard upon her discovery that his family had money, helped herself to some of the tepid coffee, then went upstairs too. In her present mood Conrad had about as much charm for her as a tadpole in a pond.

Still, there were people who loved and collected tadpoles. Perhaps that was something that she ought not to forget. And tadpoles, if they survived the hazards of pond life, eventually changed into frogs, which were rather endearing creatures, with faint fairy-tale memories clinging to them, dim possibilities that they in their turn might turn into princes . . .

Unfortunately, however, what the thought of a frog brought to Susan's mind was not a spellbound prince, but the first dissection that she had ever witnessed, in a biology class, years ago, at school. There the frog had lain, on his back, with his front neatly slit open and pinned back, so that he looked like a little green gentleman advertising a new sort of underwear. A very interesting spectacle. Susan had been fascinated. But then an appalling thing had happened. The frog's intestines had writhed. The teacher had hurriedly assured the horror-struck class of schoolgirls that the frog was dead, completely dead, but Susan, for one, had not believed her. She had been convinced that he was being crucified alive. And even if she understood such things better now, she had never forgotten that first revulsion.

Her bedroom window was open and the sky that she could see from it still had the greenish tinge of twilight. The white curtains stirred a little in a faint movement of the air. Without turning on the light in the room, Susan crossed to the window and leant on the sill. The breeze touched her face gently, cooling her cheeks, which were stinging with the flush of nervous fatigue. How long she stayed there dreaming, ten minutes, half an hour, she did not know. A nursery jingle kept running through her head. 'A frog he would a-wooing go, Whether his mother would let him or no, With a rowly-powly, gammon and spinach . . .' Garden scents and the scents of woodland and bracken drifted up to her. Somewhere among the trees an owl hooted, of course not Orlando, taking his evening exercise with Rob, since by now Rob would have settled down in the studio with the new falcon on his fist, the two of them beginning their long trial of will-power. He would not be out wandering in the woods. The owl must be a wild one, after prey.

There was a light in the window of the cottage at the corner. The light looked unusually bright because of all the whiteness in the room. There was no one to be seen inside.

Then suddenly, in the shaft of light that slanted across the garden from the window almost to the gate, Susan saw that a figure was standing. She could not see who it was or even tell if it was a man or a woman. All that she saw clearly were a head and shoulders, the head unusually large and bulbous, jutting up out of the shadows and remarkably still. That utter stillness suddenly terrified her. To be so rigid, so intent, so silent, could only mean evil. She wanted to shout out to Jocelyn, to warn him of the watcher in the garden.

Then something happened in the cottage which made her forget the figure outside. Two people moved quickly across the lighted square of the window. One was a woman. She was wearing a coat and headscarf and she was moving backwards with one arm thrown up defensively before her face. The other

91

person was Jocelyn. Of that there was no doubt. Susan saw him clearly. But he was doing something that Susan would never have believed possible, could never have imagined of him in the ugliest of nightmares. He was hitting the woman across the face. Susan saw three blows land before the woman slid down out of sight below the frame of the window.

For an instant then Jocelyn stood still. He looked down. There was a strange air of passivity, of peace about him. Then he turned swiftly in the direction of the kitchen door and vanished through it.

8

Susan found herself at the bottom of the stairs before she realised that her headlong rush down them had been only because she had had to get away from what she had seen from the window.

Opening the door, she took a few steps out into the darkness, stood still, took a deep breath and tried to stop shaking. From here she could not see the cottage at all. It was hidden by a curtain of drooping laburnum branches. But now at the gate before her, opening it and coming in, she saw the figure with the great bulbous head that she had seen in the cottage garden.

It was only Conrad in his crash-helmet.

'You weren't thinking of going over there, were you?' he asked.

She leant against the doorpost. 'No.' It was the last thing that she wanted to do.

'Where were you going then?'

'Nowhere special.'

Conrad took off the helmet and pushed his fingers through his sandy hair.

'She's all right, you know,' he said. 'He didn't really hurt her.'

In her relief, the impulse to scold which Conrad so often roused in Susan took over. 'What were you doing there, anyway, spying on them? I saw you in the garden, staring in at the window. Right in at the window!'

'Isn't that what you were doing too?'

'I was just looking out of my own window.'

'Well, aren't you glad I was there, so that I can tell you the man isn't a murderer?'

'But what were you doing there?' She asked it less suspiciously, almost humbly, this time. She was just beginning to feel gratitude with astonishing intensity.

He answered, 'I went to the gate with that woman – Sandra's mother. We talked for a bit. Then she went up to the cottage. I saw that much, but I didn't see her go in. It was odd. There was a light inside. If the door had opened, I'd have seen it. But she just seemed to vanish. So I went into the garden after her. I thought perhaps she'd collapsed there and that someone ought to be looking after her. She was in a fairly awful state, when I talked to her.'

'I know.'

'I thought perhaps she'd found that going into the cottage was more than she could stand and done a faint or something. And then when I was half-way to the door I saw what you saw.'

'She may have gone round to the kitchen door. Jocelyn may have let her in there.'

Conrad swung his helmet by its strap. He watched it with concentration as if the way it moved might determine, like a kind of lottery, what answer he should give. That he had several possible answers in his mind was obvious.

At last he said, 'I'm not sure, you know, that she was the woman you saw with Riscoe.'

'But you were there, you must have seen who she was.'

'I saw a woman in a coat and headscarf.'

'But weren't they the same coat and headscarf?'

'I'm not sure. The light was behind her. She was just a dark shape. I took for granted it was Mrs Collis. But I was so startled by what happened, I didn't keep my head. I rushed up to the door and tried to get in and shouted out to ask if she was all right. And immediately the light went out and she answered, 'I'm perfectly all right, thank you. Please go away, whoever you are.' And of course, when I looked in at the window it was dark inside and I couldn't see a thing. I went round to the back, but it was all dark there too and nobody answered when I banged on the door.'

'Why do you think it wasn't Mrs Collis?' Susan said.

'The voice. Cool as a cucumber. Educated. And the words she used. Not Mrs Collis's vocabulary at all.'

'You think it was Annette, don't you? Jocelyn's wife.'

94

'It could have been,' Conrad said.

Susan had started to shake again. It was difficult to keep the shaking out of her voice, although she did not know why she minded so much more the thought that it had been Annette whom she had seen Jocelyn strike down than that it had been Mrs Collis.

'Then what was Mrs Collis doing?' she asked. 'Where did she vanish to?'

'I don't know.'

'Don't you think she went round to the back door and Jocelyn let her in and she went into hysterics and he hit her to bring her round . . .' Her voice faded. She did not believe a word of it. 'All the same, where *did* she go, if she wasn't in there?'

'You understand, I'm not saying it wasn't Mrs Collis in there,' Conrad replied, 'only that I'm not sure it was.'

'All right, where did she go?'

'Just wandering around in a sort of daze, I should think. Perhaps she stumbled over the python.'

It made Susan want to shriek something in his face, not anything in particular, just something violent and wild. Dragging in the python now was the last straw. However, aware of Arthur and Fiona in the house behind her, wanting their night's rest, she spoke in a tone of deadly quiet. 'I thought you believed there wasn't a python.'

'That was just a theory.'

'And don't you believe in it any more?'

'I don't, as a matter of fact.'

'And you never did, did you?'

'Not really. But as a theory it had a sort of attractiveness. I had to try it out on you. I'm sorry, Susan, but that's the way my mind works. I can't help it. It isn't that I've too much imagination, it's that I've too little. I can't really think about a thing at all until I talk about it or write about it.'

Susan gave him a distracted look, which moved from his pale, eager face to the darkness around them, which all of a sudden seemed to be full of writhing serpents, of spotted snakes with double tongues, of old man Satan himself, of a hinting and whispering of evil.

'I think we ought to go and look for her,' she said.

'All right. But perhaps if we're going up against a python we ought to have a weapon of some sort. A garden hoe or something like that.'

'And a torch.'

'I've a torch in the tool-kit on the bike.'

'There'll be a hoe in the tool-shed at the back.' Susan knew that the shed was not kept locked and that there were several hoes of different shapes and sizes there.

They took a hoe each, choosing the heaviest. The slender shaft of light from Conrad's torch, sliding ahead of them as they went out to the road, cleared the darkness of a good deal of its fearsomeness. They started to call 'Mrs Collis!'

At first they called softly, then more loudly, going as far as the cottage gate and calling again. Then they happened to turn and look at one another and both began to giggle rather foolishly.

'We'll never find her like this,' Conrad said.

'I suppose she doesn't want to be found.'

'It was probably her in the cottage all the time.'

'Well, was it or wasn't it?' Susan was beginning to feel her usual exasperation with him coming on again. 'Can't you make up your mind?'

'No, I can't,' he said. 'I can only say I don't think it was. And we shan't find her like this.'

'What's happened to her, then?' She looked at the cottage. The downstairs window was dark, but there was a light in the room above, behind a curtain.

'What you said,' Conrad said. 'She tried the front door, didn't get an answer, went round to the back, then – well, perhaps then she found herself looking in through the kitchen window at a row between Riscoe and his wife and decided it wasn't the right moment for visiting.'

'And then? What did she do then?'

'Slipped away quietly to catch the bus back into town.'

It was the common-sense answer. Susan had already thought of it for herself. Yet she did not want to accept it. It set her thinking too vividly of what she had seen through the cottage window, of that strange air of quiet and appeasement with which Jocelyn had stood looking at the woman he had struck down. The new thought made Susan's flesh crawl.

'If the trouble is—' Conrad began. He was looking at her intently. With their eyes accustomed to the darkness, they could see each other's faces quite clearly, could read meaning into a frown or tightened lips. He hesitated and started again differently. 'If you're simply feeling restless and that you've got to be doing something, why don't we get on the bike and go into Swelsden and have coffee somewhere? That's what I feel like doing myself. I could manage some fish and chips too. I seem to have been missing out on regular meals lately.'

Susan was about to say no automatically, simply because of her habit of saying no to Conrad. But then she realised that the suggestion was really a very good one. It would get her away from this hag-ridden spot, and just then that was what she wanted more than anything else in the world. And even the thought of fish and chips began to seem tempting. She had had time, since her supper of bread and cheese, to recover her normally healthy hunger.

'Where's the bike?' she asked.

'Outside your gate.'

'All right, let's go.'

No one could have looked more astonished than Conrad. It was probably the first time that Susan had accepted a suggestion of his without prolonged argument. He even opened his mouth, but closed it again without saying anything and turned back towards the Lasletts' house.

At that moment something huge and black came flying at them out of the trees.

Susan gave a shriek and grabbed Conrad's arm. From its sudden rigidity she knew that he was as startled as she was, but he waved his hoe wildly at the creature and it swerved and went past just over their heads in eerily silent flight.

She gave a shaky laugh. 'It's only an owl.'

'But God, what a monster! Almost big enough to be that damned great thing they keep up at the farm.'

'The eagle owl. Orlando wouldn't be out loose. If Rob had him

97

out, he'd be on a creance. It was just an ordinary brown owl, I expect. They always look bigger than normal in the darkness.'

'They're creepy creatures, too. That headless look. Well, let's go.'

They started up the road.

Conrad's motor bicycle was just beyond the Lasletts' gate. He and Susan left the hoes in the ditch there, straddled the bicycle and set off. The rush of air past their faces felt soothing to Susan's strung-up nerves as well as cooling her cheeks. She wondered briefly if Fiona and Arthur would discover that she was not in the house and, if so, whether the two of them would worry about her unnecessarily. A note, left on the hall table, to tell them that she was not out in the woods alone, being strangled, would perhaps have been considerate. But she had not yet reached an age when the worrying about her of other people ever seemed anything but an insidious and peculiarly irritating form of restriction. Anyway, it was too late to do anything about it now. She did not suggest turning back.

The town of Swelsden engulfed them gradually, at first only with lit-up tentacles of suburban buildings that curved out between the few dark and empty fields that still remained near the town. The roads were quiet, lined with quiet houses, where the children had been put to bed hours ago and the cars put away in the garages and the parents settled down to play bridge or watch television for the rest of the evening. Then there were more houses, older, grimier, built in fairly grim terraces, though generally with a little Victorian fantasy about them, Gothic stained-glass windows, or battlemented porches. Many of the houses here had been turned into blocks of flats or boarding-houses; there was more traffic on the move; cars were parked closely along both sides of the streets and there were plenty of children about, living dangerously and to the danger of the passing motorist. The pubs and the cinemas had closed but there were still lights in a few cafés and fish-and-chip shops.

At last, in the centre of the town, came statelier houses, mostly offices now, the Georgian heart of Swelsden, built around a square in the middle of which there stood a statue of a man on a horse. He was dressed in a Roman toga and had a laurel wreath on his head. The observer had to go close to read the worn lettering on the pediment to discover that this was William III.

What William of Orange was doing in a Roman toga in the middle of a square in Swelsden it would have been difficult to guess, but there he had been for more than two centuries, often with a pigeon, or sometimes even a seagull from the nearby coast, perched on his head.

Some statues can wear birds on their heads with a certain insouciance, almost an air of gaiety, a sort of, 'Look at clever me, balancing this thing on my head!' But not poor, serious William. He only looked uneasy and afraid of seeming ridiculous.

The café to which Conrad took Susan was in one of the narrow side-streets leading into the old square. The table-tops were of cream-coloured plastic, the seats vermilion. On the menu the fried haddock and chips had been metamorphosed into seafood and french fries. The coffee was the instant kind and watery at that.

But there was an air of drowsy calm about the place. Young couples who had been to the cinema sat and dreamed into one another's eyes. Tired old people who were waiting for the last bus home sat over single cups of tea, trying to make them last until it was time to get on to their weary feet again and shuffle out to the bus-stop. The waitress was elderly and abstracted, but she was kind. Bringing Susan and Conrad their plates of fish and chips and bottles of tomato sauce and vinegar, she said it was a hot night, wasn't it, and one was always complaining, wasn't one, wet or shine, and her dim smile was sweet, with that peculiar gentleness that the lonely and unappreciated often reserve for lovers, who of all people do not need it.

Susan and Conrad, however, were not lovers. Susan, indeed, had already lost most of the feeling of gratitude to Conrad with which she had started on the ride into Swelsden. Certain awkward questions had formed in her mind and as soon as the waitress had left them she began to ask these.

'Conrad, you really meant what you said about the python, did you? You've decided it exists.'

He speared a chip on his fork.

'I've told you I never really thought it didn't,' he said.

'Yes, I know, and you told me that's how your mind works,' Susan said. 'So far as I can see, it works in whatever way happens to be the most convenient at the moment. But the important question now is, is there any evidence either way? Since it was you who raised the doubt in the first place, don't you think you might settle it with something a little more definite than just the workings of your mind? For instance, could you tell me if anyone besides Rob and Nina saw the python?'

'Oh yes,' Conrad said. 'The Merrows did.'

'The—?' For the moment Susan had forgotten the name. 'Oh, the Merrows, the children who threw the brick.'

'And their mother,' Conrad said. 'After that incident I went along to the village and had a talk to her. She says she saw the python when it arrived. Rob Riscoe brought it in a sort of hamper from London and Mrs Merrow saw him bundle the thing out of the hamper into the cage he'd prepared for it, "Just as if it was a bundle of wet washing as couldn't up and squeeze him to death." That's how she put it. She nearly had a fit on the spot and told Nina that if that thing was staying around Nina needn't count on seeing her any more. But Nina calmed her down by showing her how safe and strong the cage was and saying she didn't much care for snakes herself but her husband had set his heart on having one and so she meant to try to get used to this one. And Mrs Merrow was always ready to do anything on earth for Mr Riscoe – as most women seem to be, for some reason I don't entirely understand – and so she agreed to go on helping Nina out for his sake, so long as she need never even look at the python, because even looking at it did things to her.' He grinned. 'D'you know the Emily Dickinson thing about a snake?

> "Several of nature's people
> I know and they know me;
> I feel for them a transport
> Of cordiality;
>
> But never met this fellow,
> Attended or alone,

100

Without a tighter breathing,
And zero at the bone." '

'Or, as Mr Burke, the bobby, said, "There's something about snakes," ' said Susan.

'Exactly. But before Mrs Merrow's next visit to Bright's Farm was due, you see, the python had disappeared.'

'And she told her children it had strangled Sandra?'

'It seems so.'

'Out of malice, or really believing it?'

'Oh, really believing it. I shouldn't think there's an ounce of malice in the woman's body. She seemed to me to be one of those strange, utterly unenvious, almost saintly working-class women whom women like Nina and your sister rely on to help keep them sane through all the awful complexities of middle-class life.'

Susan gave him a surprised look across a forkful of fried haddock. For once he looked a little self-conscious. He went on quickly, 'What I meant is, Mrs Merrow is a thoroughly nice person. She liked the Riscoes, she didn't like the python, but she was ready to face working in its neighbourhood for Rob Riscoe's sake. And she did most definitely see the thing. So that idea of mine that perhaps the Riscoes only invented one because they wanted the police to come and find lots more bodies in the woods, or something of that sort, was all wet. It was just one of my more undisciplined flights of fancy. All the same . . .'

He paused there, frowning.

'The children who threw the brick, Conrad,' Susan said, 'they really were there too, were they? They weren't just an undisciplined flight of fancy?'

'What makes you think they were?'

'Arthur didn't see them.'

His coffee-cup was half-way to his mouth. He set it down slowly. Slowly his face grew paler and his freckles darker and muddier.

'That means one of us is lying, doesn't it? Take your pick.'

'I didn't mean—'

'Oh yes, you did.' Conrad suddenly began to sound cheerful

about it. The corners of his mouth went up in a fierce, happy little smile. Being accused of lying might have been something he found remarkably stimulating. 'You think I heaved that brick through the window myself. Fine, but will you tell me what I did it for? Bitterness at the loss of my old home? Desire to create some news for the *Swelsden Weekly Advertiser*, out of sheer gratitude for the enormous salary they pay me? The pure joy of brick-throwing?'

'I suppose that's what sounds the likeliest,' Susan said, beginning to smile too. 'It's nice, throwing things. But what really did happen? That's what I can't understand, assuming both of you are telling the truth.'

'But one of us can't be. One of us is telling a thumping lie. There's no way round it.'

He was enjoying himself now, preparing to tease her and puzzle her into losing her temper. It occurred to her that any woman who settled down to the job of living with Conrad would have to learn enormous self-control.

Though this was not a future that she was planning for herself, she controlled herself carefully now. 'What's your version of what happened, true or false, from beginning to end?' she asked.

He extracted a haddock bone from between his teeth.

'It's one of my nightmares that some day I'll have to stand up in court somewhere and tell a judge and a jury and a roomful of other people about something I saw, or they think I saw, and that someone's life or liberty may depend on what I say, when all the time I was thinking so hard about something quite different that I never really noticed what happened at all.'

'You mean you *didn't* see those children throw the brick?'

'No, I don't mean that. I did see them. Well, more or less. But you wanted my story from beginning to end, so I was starting at the real beginning. I went out this morning, you see, hoping I could get you to come out for the day with me, go to the sea perhaps, swim . . . I went to your sister's house and there was nobody there. I went on to the Taylors' – Jocelyn Riscoe's cottage. There was nobody there. So I thought perhaps you were all up at the farm and I might as well try there too. I rode up the lane to the house and all the time I was thinking about you and whether or not you'd come to the sea with me and I suppose the kids heard the bike, because by the time I got there they were running as hard as they could for the wood. And there was a great hole in the sitting-room window and half a brick on the ground. So of course I took for granted they'd thrown it. I picked it up to look at it, but I was still thinking about you, and the next thing I knew, your brother-in-law had me by the throat. And I suppose it's just possible he really didn't see the children. I'd say he must have, but if you want to believe him as well as me, all right, he didn't, he was too excited. He's a little past the age for jumping out of windows and seizing people by the throat and trying to shake their teeth out.'

'Arthur isn't as old as all that,' Susan said, 'and he's extremely strong and fast when he moves. He played rugger at school, and he was in the army for a time and he's always made a thing of physical fitness. He was out of that window before the rest of us had even begun to realise what had happened.'

'You might go on and ask me why he should say he hadn't seen the children if he had.'

'Well, why did he?'

Conrad leant back on his vermilion chair. 'That's what I'm asking myself. He may not like me much, but I can't really see him going to such lengths just to discredit me for my own sake, so to speak. No, the way I told the story just now must be the right one. His mind was on something else and he simply didn't see the kids.'

'Is that what you really think now, or are you just trying it out on me to see how it sounds?'

'Well, I told you that's how my mind works. I have to try things out on someone else to find out what I think about them. There's something else I was thinking of trying out on you ...' But instead of going on, he seemed abruptly to withdraw from her, to lose himself in some troubling thoughts which she felt instinctively had nothing to do with her.

She let him brood, finding the silence welcome. Her coffee was almost cold but she finished it, put her elbows on the table and rested her head on her hands. A moment later she realised that she had just decided not to go on with the typing for Rob and

Nina, not to return to the farm in the morning, not to see Jocelyn again and not, if possible, ever to meet Annette. Tomorrow she would pack up her books and go back to London.

What had made her reach this decision in this sudden way she did not know. She supposed that it had been growing in her ever since she had seen Jocelyn turn into someone whom she had never met before, someone, she felt very sure, whom she wanted never to meet again. In any case, she was going back to London tomorrow. And this evening she would get Conrad to drop her off at Bright's Farm so that she could go in and tell Nina, with suitable apologies, that she would have to do the rest of her typing herself.

9

Susan was aware, as she turned these things over in her mind, that Conrad had started talking again. She had not listened, but now something that he said penetrated her self-absorption.

'. . . and the job actually stopped a month ago and I only stayed on because I heard you were coming.'

'The job?' Susan said. 'Your job with the *Advertiser*? Have you been sacked?'

'You weren't listening, were you?' He smiled. 'Well, you're tired as hell. I can see that. I shouldn't have been bothering you with the story.'

'I'm sorry, it's true I was miles away,' she said. 'Try again.'

'I was telling you I'm not on the *Advertiser* any more, that's all. You don't think even the *Advertiser* would have stood for the way I've been hanging round for the last few days, do you? Actually, they've a very small and badly paid staff whom they overwork atrociously and who only stick it because they're too old and doddery to dare to look for jobs elsewhere, or so young and uneducated they don't know how they're being exploited. I only stayed on as long as I did to please my mother, because she thought it was a fine old family business and she'd been very clever to get me into something where she saw me ending up as a director. And then I stayed because the *Daily Post* thing came along. I've been their Swelsden correspondent for the last few months. That doesn't sound much but I thought with luck I might turn it into something useful. As I have. Suddenly, out of the blue, they offered me this job in London.'

'But that sounds wonderful, Conrad! You must have impressed them terrifically.'

'Yes,' he agreed without humility. 'But the job doesn't start till next month, and I'd got some money saved up so I decided to give myself a holiday, and I knew you were coming to the Lasletts, so I thought I'd take the holiday here. And then this business about Taylor blew up and I thought I might do myself some good with the *Post* if I followed it up . . .' He paused, giving her an uncertain look. 'I haven't told you much about that. I'm not talking about the murder. I mean a thing I saw out there one evening.'

'You mean your suspicion that Taylor was hiding out after robbing a bank,' Susan replied. 'You did say something about it, but it was all awfully vague and I thought you were making it up as you went along. Do you mean you found out something real about him?'

'Yes.'

She was watching his face carefully. 'It's funny,' she said, 'I don't know why it is I never believe anything you tell me. I can't think of any real reason for it. It's purely automatic. I'm awfully glad, though, about the *Post*. Congratulations.'

'Thank you. Now this thing I know about Taylor – I haven't told anyone else about it yet, because I was saving it up until I knew a bit more. But now, because of Sandra, there's the question of whether I oughtn't to tell the police.'

'Go on. What is it?'

'Well, I think Taylor and Rob Riscoe are involved together in something pretty peculiar. I rather think it's smuggling of some sort.'

She stared at him as if he had gone mad. 'Taylor and *Rob*?'

'Wait!' he said quickly. 'Let me tell you what I saw, then pull it to pieces as much as you like. But I swear to you this is what I saw. I swear it solemnly. So don't jump to the conclusion this time that I'm making it up. I was up near the farm one evening, fairly late. I often went out there and wandered about. I suppose it was a way of trying to get adjusted to the fact that it all belonged to somebody else. At first I used to find it rather difficult to believe and I've never quite got rid of the feeling that I've a sort of right to be there. Well, I was on that open ground behind the cottage. You know there's a big v-shaped meadow there where there are sometimes a few sheep. I was at the edge of it, in the shadow of the trees, and it was dusk, which is why Taylor didn't see me when he came out of the cottage and walked out into the middle of the field and stood there for a time. He seemed to be listening for something, and kept looking up into the sky. Then I heard a plane coming over. It was coming from the coast. It was coming down very low, barely skimming the trees and I thought it was going to try to land. But it just dropped something and sheered off. The thing came down on a little parachute and Taylor ran forward to get it. But Riscoe was there first. I hadn't noticed him till then. He'd been standing quite near me all the time, with that owl of his on his fist. I don't know if he saw me or not. He went out very quickly and quietly – you know that smooth, silent way he has of moving – and when Taylor got to the place where the package fell, Riscoe was there waiting for him. They stood talking for a minute or two, then Taylor picked the thing up and they went back to the cottage together.'

He stopped as if he were expecting a comment. Susan said nothing.

'That was about three weeks ago,' he added.

'And is that all?'

'Well no, there's what happened next.'

'Go on, then.'

'I don't mean that evening. I hung about for a time and saw Riscoe come out and go home and then the lights in the cottage went out, so I went home too. But it was after that that I really began to keep an eye on the Taylors and one day Nina Riscoe told me they were leaving. So I thought I understood what had happened that night. I thought Riscoe had caught Taylor out in some smuggling operation and had a quiet talk with him, telling him that if he'd get out of the cottage without any fuss, he'd hear no more about the matter, as far as Riscoe was concerned.'

'But why should Rob have done that? Wouldn't he have gone to the police?'

'There's his nature, you see,' Conrad said. 'You know the only things he cares about are those birds of his, and that's given him almost a mania for peace and quiet. He hates noise and fuss. He likes to be left alone by people. And when a person's like that, he can really be pretty lawless underneath. He may not want to do anything criminal himself, but he doesn't mind it much when somebody else does, so long as it doesn't affect him himself. And so it might be that the first thing Riscoe thought of when he caught Taylor was not how to stop an illegal activity, but how to get rid of Taylor before the police caught on too and came round, making a nuisance of themselves.'

'But in the end that's led to far worse trouble than just the police asking questions about Taylor,' Susan said.

'Riscoe wasn't to know that, was he? He didn't know – I mean if that first idea I had was right – that Taylor was sick of Sandra and was going to do her in, leaving her body practically at Riscoe's back door.'

'But Taylor didn't do her in. The police have said it again and again. With that withered arm, he couldn't have throttled anybody.'

'No, I know.'

Susan felt that she was being stupid. She felt that all the time that Conrad had been talking, he had really been telling her something quite different from what he had seemed to be saying. But she was too tired and confused and depressed to grasp what it was. Usually she was quick, all too quick, to read second meanings into Conrad's complex utterances. But tonight the fogginess of a kind of indifference obscured them. Ever since she had seen Jocelyn, the sensitive, quiet, gifted man whom she had loved with such painful intensity, turn in front of her eyes into a monster, nothing had felt worth the effort of understanding.

'You'd better spell the rest of it out for me,' she said wearily. 'You haven't said it all yet, have you? Personally, I don't see . . .' She stopped, because suddenly she did see. A nervous chill went through her and patches of angry scarlet appeared on her cheeks. 'Yes, I do see what you've been leading up to. You mean if Rob was in this thing with Taylor, if they were partners, if that's why they talked so calmly and quietly when they met in the middle of the meadow and then went back to the cottage together—'

108

'And decided to pack it in,' Conrad interrupted, 'because Riscoe had seen me watching—'

'Yes, well, then – then they also decided to get rid of Sandra, because Taylor was sick of her and she knew too much about them just to be turned loose. So they – Rob – killed her – since it couldn't have been Taylor.' Susan leant across the table and spat the words at him. 'You horrible little worm, you're saying Rob killed Sandra!'

He started to draw a picture in the congealing fat left on his plate by the fish and chips.

'How does it sound?' he asked.

'*Sound?*' She said it so loudly and shrilly that several people looked round at them. Drawing a deep breath, she carefully lowered her voice. 'Is any of this true, Conrad, any of it at all?'

'What I told you I saw is true,' he answered. 'The rest of it is just me trying to think things out clearly.'

'And you've said nothing at all about it to the police?'

'Not yet.'

'Why not?'

Once she started to think about it, she began to think that one of the most astonishing parts of the story was that Conrad had said nothing to the police. He had no close ties that she knew of with the Riscoes, had no reason to want to protect them.

He answered, 'Because to begin with I thought I was on to something exciting and that if I kept on watching I might come up with something pretty dramatic. Then when the Taylors left I thought I understood what had happened. I mean, that Riscoe had got rid of them quietly for the sake of his own peace and quiet. And I had a good deal of sympathy with him, besides those feelings we all have that some things aren't our business, which generally speaking make survival on this earth possible. And then when they found Sandra's body it took me a little while to think things out even as far as I have, and since then – well, I've been wanting to talk to you before I did anything, and this has really been my first opportunity.'

Susan had no answer. Perhaps if she had trusted him more she would have known what to say, but she could not get rid of the feeling that perhaps there had never been any meeting of Rob

109

and Taylor in the middle of the field, perhaps no plane flying low, or any mysterious parcel dropped by parachute.

She looked up at the clock above the counter where the tired-eyed waitress stood behind the tea-urn, staring vacantly across the room. The clock had a tired and vacant look as well, ticking the minutes jerkily away with hands stiffened as if by arthritis. Susan and Conrad were almost the last customers.

'It's late, they're longing for us to go,' she said.

'You haven't told me what you think I ought to do,' he said.

'I don't know,' she said. 'I'll think. Ring me up tomorrow . . . No, don't. I shan't be there. I'm going back to London.'

'Tomorrow?' He stared at her in shocked disbelief. 'You can't go in the middle of all this.'

'The police haven't told me not to.'

Conrad stood up and went over to the counter to pay the waitress. She gave him a sad look, as if, as lovers, he and Susan had not quite given her her money's worth. Looking sulky, he strode out of the door ahead of Susan and almost let it swing shut in her face.

But out in the quiet street he turned back to her with a sympathetically perceptive look that she had not expected.

'It's what you saw through that window that's decided you, isn't it?' he said. 'I don't think myself you ought to worry too much about it. Men often hit women, and women men, without doing one another any mortal harm. But if you feel so strongly about it, you're probably right to go away.'

'The trouble is,' Susan said, as they fell into step, walking to where Conrad had parked the motor bike, 'I said I'd do that typing for Nina . . . Conrad, could you take me there now? I could take the manuscript with me and finish it at home.'

'Isn't it rather late for a call?'

'They're late people. They may even not go to bed at all to-night. Rob's waking the falcon and I believe Nina stays up when he does it to make tea for him and so on. If there aren't any lights on in the house and it looks as if they've gone to bed, we needn't stop.'

'All right.' He settled himself on the saddle of the motor bike and kicked the starter. 'I'll take you there. You're a rum girl,

110

Susan, worrying about that typing at a time like this. You don't like to let people down, do you? Yet if I go to the police with my yarn, the Riscoes are going to have a lot more to think about than that manuscript.'

These were words so nearly prophetic that a time came when Susan almost convinced herself that she had heard something ominous in them at the time. Something at least wedged them in her memory, to be shaken loose into her consciousness later. But the truth was that as she crouched behind Conrad's bent figure on the motor bike, holding on to his waist, she did not go on thinking about what he had said, but of the problem of why she did not trust him more, found him so impossible to take seriously.

It had something to do with their first few meetings, a year ago. He had made such a thing about falling in love with her at first sight, and people simply didn't fall in love at first sight, she believed, not with her at any rate. Sometimes they had with Fiona, or they had said they had, or Fiona had said that they had said they had, and certainly she had become very radiant and cheerful through believing it. But Susan had been born sceptical. If she had been able to talk at the time, she would probably have told the doctor who delivered her and said that she was a fine baby that he was exaggerating absurdly.

And to be told by Conrad that he had fallen in love with her at first sight, that he had never loved anyone else in the same way before and never would again, had only made her feel embarrassed and rather resentful. How could he possibly have imagined she was such a fool as to swallow that? If he had put it flatly in terms of desire, had simply told her how urgently he wanted her, she thought that she would have had more regard for him. But the wretched boy always had to dramatise everything, make it twopence coloured where plain would have been so much more appropriate. So you ended up not exactly thinking him a liar, yet never quite believing him about anything.

Her own falling in love with Jocelyn had been at first sight, of course, but still, she had not known it at the time. It had simply happened to her and immediately, as it were, gone underground, to emerge into the light again a little way at a time, very

111

quietly, very tentatively. Indeed, she had never felt quite certain that the state of emotion that he had created in her was the state called being in love until she knew that she had lost him.

The lights had not been turned out at Bright's Farm. They shone down the lane, one from the kitchen, another from behind the fanlight over the front door, another from the studio. That puzzled Susan. It also puzzled her, as she and Conrad approached the house, that the light from the studio should be so bright. She knew that in the early stage of training a hawk or falcon it was usual to have only a dim light in the room, or the bird would become unmanageably scared and aggressive. It puzzled her too that the door through which the light was streaming out should be wide open. Normally, if Rob had been waking the falcon, the door would have been shut.

The next unexpected thing that Susan saw was that the door of the owl's cage was wide open and that Orlando was not inside it. But it was only when Conrad switched off the engine of the motor bike that she heard the screaming coming from the studio.

They ran towards it.

Inside they saw Sandra's mother, standing on a chair, her thin legs pressed close together, her hands clutching her skirt tightly round her. It was she who was screaming, while her eyes bulged with terror out of her paper-white face.

All around her the floor seethed with a sea of white rats and mice. Perhaps the number of them was not really so great, but because of the way they darted here and there, tumbling distractedly over one another, their ruby eyes flashing and long tails twitching, the place seemed to be alive with them. And in the old leather-covered armchair which had its back to the door, in the bright light of the table lamp behind him, sat Rob, doing nothing. He sat crookedly, leaning right over to one side, and he was apparently looking without emotion at the hysterically bewildered rodents round him and the screaming woman.

But when Susan and Conrad came further into the room they saw that he was not really looking at anything. Somehow the side of his head had been smashed in and he was dead.

112

10

It was the woman's screaming that at first seemed the most unbearable part of the nightmare and kept Susan rooted where she was. The noise was hideous. At the same time it felt like an obscene expression of her own feelings. Yet she had never felt any horror or disgust at rats or mice and Rob, dead in the chair, did not seem to have anything to do with Rob.

Conrad went forward, the tide of rats and mice receding terrified before him and sweeping in a churning stream through the door from which they must have emerged when their cages were opened. He went close to Rob, stood looking down at him, then put out a tentative hand and touched his wrist.

It was his left wrist, which hung down over the edge of the broad arm of the chair. His right arm was bent under his slumped body. He had fallen to the right under the murderous blows that had crashed on to the left side of his head. The side of his face was a pulpy mass of blood and bone. A stream of blood had gushed down his neck and chest and coagulated in the wool of his pullover and there were splashes over the back of the chair. He must have died very quickly.

At Conrad's touch Rob's arm seemed to move of itself and Conrad snatched his hand away. A small white, pink-eyed thing, a mouse, slid out from the cuff of Rob's shirt-sleeve, scampered down his legs and fled to join the others. At that Susan began to scream. She only screamed once, because she jammed her fingers into her mouth, but the noise went on and on in her head.

Conrad turned on her, took her by the shoulders and shook her. His freckles stood out lividly against the whiteness of his face and made her think of the splashes of dried blood on Rob's shirt.

'He's dead,' Conrad said. 'He's stone cold. We've got to get the police.'

Susan nodded but kept her fingers in her mouth to stop the noise coming out.

Mrs Collis stopped screaming and made a queer rattling noise instead. It was her teeth chattering. She was still on the chair, holding her coat closely round her knees.

'Will you go, or shall I?' Conrad asked Susan. He spoke slowly and very distinctly as if to a deaf person or a halfwit, his finger-tips digging into her shoulders. 'One of us ought to stay here with – her.'

'I'll go,' Susan said and sprang away to the door before he could question it.

She was half-way down the drive before she thought that of course he had meant her to go straight into the house and tele-phone from there. It would have been far quicker than running all the way to the Lasletts'. But if she had gone into the farm-house she would have had to face Nina, rouse her, perhaps, if she had gone to bed or fallen asleep in the chair while Rob sat waking the falcon, perhaps break the news of his death to her. Susan ran on.

She had a key to the front door in a pocket of her jacket. In the mood when extreme nervous tension produces not clumsiness but remarkable surety of action, she shot the key straight into the lock without any fumbling, threw the door open and would have gone straight to the telephone if she had not come face to face at the foot of the stairs with a frantic-looking Fiona.

'You did it again!' Fiona cried. She was in her dressing-gown. Her hair was tumbled. She grabbed at Susan's arm, shaking it. 'You went off alone without a word to us! Can't you ever think of other people? We've been wild with worry.'

'I wasn't alone, I was with Conrad, and you'd gone to bed. Look,' Susan said, 'I've got to telephone—'

'How were we to know you were with Conrad?' Fiona was barring the way to the telephone. 'How do we know, if it comes to that, that Conrad isn't the murderer? He's a very strange

114

young man. What do we really know about him? We don't know anything. And you go off like that without a word—'

'I thought you'd gone to bed. Please, Fiona—'

'We did go to bed, but neither of us could get to sleep so I got up after a bit to make a hot drink and I saw your bedroom door was open and that you hadn't gone to bed at all and then I found you weren't anywhere else in the house either.'

'Listen, I've got to phone the police.' Susan thrust Fiona firmly out of her way, making for the telephone. When Susan exerted her strength, she was a good deal the stronger of the sisters. 'How do you dial them here? Is it 999?'

From the top of the stairs, Arthur said, 'Yes. I'll do it for you, if you'll tell me what's happened.'

He came down the stairs, looking as straight-backed and square-shouldered in his silk dressing-gown as in his office suit. His hair was smooth and he had an open book in his hand. If, like Fiona, he had been wild with anxiety at Susan's disappearance, he did not show it.

Susan felt profoundly grateful for his calm. In an emergency there was no one on whom she would sooner rely than Arthur.

'It's Rob,' she said. 'Someone went into the studio when he was waking the falcon and hit him . . .' Her voice began to shake. 'He's dead. It was . . .' She nearly choked. 'On the head. He's dead. It was – we couldn't be wrong about it. So Conrad stayed on with Mrs Collis and I came here to telephone.'

Fiona began to ask a string of questions without leaving time for any answers. Arthur, more sensibly, asked nothing else just then but took the telephone from Susan's hand and dialled, not 999, but Mr Burke's number, told him concisely that his sister-in-law and Mr Ives had just discovered Mr Riscoe dead in his studio, that they believed his death to be murder, that Mr Ives was still in the studio and that Arthur himself would be there in a few minutes.

As he put the telephone down again and leapt up the stairs, Fiona called after him, 'I'm going with you, Arthur!'

He paused at the top to look down at Susan. 'Does Jocelyn know about this?'

'No,' she said.

115

'And Nina?'

'I don't know. I don't think so.'

'Well, wait for me. I'll get dressed and take you back to the farm in the car. That'll be quicker than walking. And Fiona can go to get Jocelyn when she's ready.'

'I'll be ready as soon as you are,' Fiona said as she flew up the stairs and vanished into their bedroom.

Susan stood waiting. She started to think of the falcon. What had happened to the falcon? And the glove, the falconer's glove, that should have been on Rob's left hand, why had it been lying on the table? Sue could visualise it clearly there, with its heavy fringed gauntlet and the old stains made by the morsels of meat with which he had fed the goshawk, while he was holding her and which never quite got cleaned away. Had Rob started to wake the peregrine, then given it up because of an interruption? Or never started it at all? He must have meant to do it, because there were newspapers on the floor all round his chair. These were for the mutes, or droppings of the falcon. But had there been any mutes on the paper? She had not noticed. She had only seen the swirling rats and mice all over the floor.

Fiona was not in fact ready as soon as Arthur. He reappeared in only a minute or two in flannel trousers and a jersey, which he had put on over his pyjamas. He took Susan's arm and hurried her out of the house, into the garage, into the car and backed this out into the road, all with an astonishing rapidity and absence of excitement which reminded Susan of his action when the brick had crashed through the Riscoes' sitting-room window. He drove the Bentley a little way past the cottage, then stopped.

'And,' he said, turning to look at Susan, 'tell me some more about it. First, what were you doing at the Riscoes' at this time of night?'

She recognised the tone of authority and for once in her life felt no resentment at it.

'I went there to tell them that I couldn't go on with their typing,' she said. 'I'd been into Swelsden with Conrad and he brought me back and I thought we could look in at the farm to see if Nina was still up.'

'Why couldn't it wait till tomorrow?'

'Oh, it could have waited, it was just that I suddenly thought . . .'
She was uncomfortably aware of the shrewdness of Arthur's gaze
and at the same time of how many things that had happened that
evening she did not want to tell him. She began to pick her
words more carefully. 'I knew Nina would probably be up, if
Rob was waking the new peregrine, and I'd just made up my
mind, you see, that I couldn't go on with the typing because I
wasn't getting any of my own work done. And I've really got to
start working hard if I want to do well next year. So I thought I'd
go and explain this to Nina while I was still feeling decided and
couldn't be talked out of it.'

Arthur gave an odd half-smile. 'There's something about all
that that doesn't sound right, Susan. It doesn't seem in character.
Let's leave it for the present. Just tell me what happened when
you got there.'

'Someone was screaming.'

'In the studio?'

'Yes, the door was wide open, and Orlando's cage was open
too and he wasn't there, and there was a light on in the studio, a
stronger light than there would have been if Rob had been
waking the falcon, and when we looked in we saw that woman,
Mrs Collis, on a chair, yelling her head off, and there were rats
and mice all over the floor. That's why she was screaming, not
because of Rob. He was there, in the armchair. . . .'

He put a hand quickly on one of hers. His was comfortingly
steady. 'All right, don't try to tell me about that. I'll see it myself
when I get there. But you're sure he was dead?'

'Oh yes, yes. Conrad said he was quite cold. He touched him
and a mouse jumped out of his sleeve and . . .' She had to press
her fingers into her mouth again. She was afraid that she was
going to vomit in the car.

Arthur gave her a moment, watching her with a puzzled expression.

'I don't understand about the owl and the other creatures,' he
said. 'Someone killed Rob, then let them all go, is that it?'

'I don't know. I suppose so.'

'What about the falcon?'

'She wasn't there. And the glove was there on the table.'

117

'What does it mean that it was there? I'm not up in falconry like you.'

'I think it means either that Rob had stopped waking her and put her back in the shed, or else that somebody deliberately let her go, like the other animals.'

'And took Rob's glove off and put it on the table after he was dead.'

'Yes.'

'What about the other one – Celia, isn't that her name? Has she been let loose?'

'The goshawk. I don't know. I'll look when we get there.'

He started up the engine again. 'And that's all you want to tell me, is it? You wouldn't like to tell me the real reason why you went to the farm so late in the evening.'

'I told you the reason, Arthur.'

He gave the same little wry smile as before. 'Not quite all of it, I'm fairly sure of that. As I said, it doesn't strike me as quite in character. You've always been a rather conscientious person. You're apt to keep your promises. So if you suddenly decided you couldn't go on with the typing you'd promised to do, it was because something happened, something fairly important. It wasn't anything Rob himself did, was it? Anything he did or said?' As the car rolled forward, he added, 'I'm not trying to pry, Susan, truly. But the police are going to put you through all this, probably quite soon. And if there's anything you really don't want them to know, think out very carefully how you go about keeping it from them, because they're pretty good at tearing a thin story to pieces.'

'There isn't a single thing about Rob and me I mind them knowing, not a single thing!'

She suddenly had a frightening feeling that she might start to laugh. Yet she knew that the sound might really have burst out of her in screams of horror or tears of fury. Some time soon, she knew, she was going to start feeling grief for Rob; grief for a man who, in spite of somehow frightening her at times, had actually never shown her anything but kindness and a remarkable degree of understanding. The threat of this grief was a darkening cloud beginning to rise up over the rim of her consciousness. But at present her mind seemed to be crammed only with jangling and unrelated fragments of what she had experienced that evening. And this preposterous suspicion about Rob and herself that Arthur seemed to share with Fiona felt for the moment like the last intolerable craziness that might drive her into helpless hysteria.

Taking a tight grip of herself, she forced herself to say calmly, 'If you want the real truth, Arthur, it's Jocelyn I've always been in love with, not Rob, but I don't see any need for the police to know that, do you?'

'Ah, I see.' She realised that his voice was gentle and not really surprised. 'No, I shouldn't think there's any need to mention it. But that's the real reason why you came round here tonight, isn't it? You'd decided you couldn't stand staying here with Jocelyn and Annette in the cottage and you were going back to London tomorrow. But being that conscientious character I was talking about, you came along to tell the Riscoes you were going, perhaps to offer to take the typing with you. Yes, I find that a lot more convincing than the other story. But, like you, I don't see any need for the police to know it.'

Once more he had startled Susan. It was astonishing to discover that her brother-in-law, whom she had always regarded as kind, stolid and sensible but a long way from bright, should have such a quick and perceptive mind as well as those unexpectedly swift physical reactions. She began to find the intensity of Fiona's love for him more understandable.

When they stopped at the door of the studio, it was still open with light streaming out. But all was silent. Conrad came out to meet them.

'So that's why you took so long,' he said to Susan. 'I thought you'd just telephone from the house here.'

'Does Nina know yet?' Arthur asked.

'Oh yes, she knows,' Conrad answered. 'She came quietly to the door a few minutes after Susan left. I was still trying to get the Collis woman to stop shrieking. And Mrs Riscoe simply stood in the doorway, looking in, and then went away. She didn't go near her husband. She didn't answer when I spoke to her. She just turned round and went back into the house. And for some reason that brought Mrs Collis to her senses. She got down from the chair and went out after Mrs Riscoe, and they're in there in the kitchen together. Are the police coming?'

'Yes.' Arthur went to the door of the studio and stood there quietly, looking in, just as Nina had, according to Conrad. After a moment Arthur said, 'Susan, why don't you go in to Nina now and see if you can do anything for her?'

'Yes, I will.'

But before Susan could go to the house, there was something which she knew she had to do. She knew that it was important. As Arthur went towards the body in the chair, islanded on sheets of newspapers, she turned to Orlando's open cage, saw his leash dangling from the perch, then went to Conrad's motor bike, extracted his torch from the tool-kit, walked quietly round the studio to the shed behind it, where Rob had kept Rosalind for the short time that he had possessed her, and tried the door.

It was unlocked. Shading the light with her hand, in case the falcon should be in there and frightened by the sudden bright-ness, Susan drew the door open a few inches and looked in. The falcon was not there. Nor was the leash, which normally would have been attached to her jesses by a steel swivel and tied her to her perch. The shed was empty.

Now there was the question of whether or not Celia, the gos-hawk, had been freed.

Susan went on to the hawk's mews, which was beyond the shed where Rosalind had been kept. The door of the mews was wide open and Celia was gone. Her hood lay on the floor. Her leash hung down from the perch to which it had been tied.

So three birds were missing, but only two leashes had been left behind.

Frowning so deeply that the lines on her forehead put apparent years on to her age, Susan at last went looking for Nina.

The kitchen, where she found her, was a high room with an uneven stone floor and only a minimum of modern conveni-ences; sink-units and dishwashers had never made much appeal to Nina's imagination. She was sitting at the table in a straight-backed chair, and was staring straight in front of her. Her hands lay folded in her lap. Except for the slight movement of her breathing, she was completely still. Touchie, the monkey, as if aware of something extremely alarming and totally beyond his comprehension in the atmosphere, cowered nervously on top of the tall dresser. Somewhere outside Oliver, the pointer, gave an occasional uneasy bark.

Mrs Collis was briskly making tea. As some women can, she had already assumed the air of knowing where everything was, the tea, the milk, the sugar, the cups and saucers. She might have been working in that kitchen for years. She had shed all signs of her recent terror.

'You'd like some tea, too,' she stated to Susan and brought a third cup out of the cupboard. 'I took one look at her—' She nodded towards Nina, 'and I said to myself, "Tea." It's the right thing for shock, I remember that from the war days. I remember my mother coming in, when the raiding was bad, and saying, "You don't give 'em brandy, you give 'em tea, hot, sweet tea. Brandy only makes them bleed worse." I was only a small kid, of course, and there's a lot about the war and the raids I don't remember, but that always stuck in my head. Kids are queer. As if I'd ever have a chance of giving anyone brandy. Yet I remember that. And the front door being blown off its hinges. I remember that, too. My father made a joke of it, said there was really no way now to keep out my boy-friends. He was a grand old boy till he started his arthritis, then his temper changed. But we were a grand family in them days. It was a happy time, the war . . .'

She chattered on, perhaps with some well-intentioned thought of taking Nina's mind off her tragedy, perhaps simply because she did not know how to stop, because, in her loneliness, she had lost the art of stopping.

Susan drew a chair close to Nina's, sat down beside her and put a hand on hers as they lay in her lap. The touch of them startled Susan, they were so icily cold.

While she was wondering whether or not to speak, Nina said in a low voice, 'I knew, of course.'

'Knew? What?' Susan asked.

'That he was dead. Earlier. Before you all came and this woman started screaming. Who is she?'

'I told her,' Mrs Collis said over her shoulder as she poured the boiling water into the teapot. ' "I'm Mrs Collis," I said, "I'm Sandra's mother." '

Nina ignored her, speaking almost in a whisper into Susan's ear. 'I knew. I went out there and found him. He was dying. I think he knew me for just a moment, then he died. I came in here, meaning to ring up the police. I can't quite remember now if I did it or not.'

'I don't think you did,' Susan said.

'No, I don't really think I did. I must just have sat down here and gone to sleep. I know I was very tired.'

'You must have fainted.'

'I never fainted in my life.'

'Some other things have happened to you today that haven't happened to you before in your life,' Mrs Collis said, putting a cup of khaki-coloured tea in front of Nina. 'Now drink that while it's hot. It'll make you feel more yourself!'

Nina obediently sipped the tea, then put the cup down again. 'I don't like sugar,' she said.

'Hot and strong and sweet,' Mrs Collis said. 'That's what you want for shock. Not brandy – I remember my mother saying it. "It only makes the bleeding worse . . ." '

Any bleeding that Nina was doing, Susan thought, was being done internally.

'Nina, was it you who let all the animals out?' she asked softly.

'Animals?' Nina said vaguely.

'The rats and mice and the birds – they've all been freed. Did you do it?'

'Of course not,' Nina said.

'Who did it, then?'

'Does it matter? I'd have got rid of them anyway. I'll keep Touchie and Oliver, but I'd have got rid of all the others.'

'You're sure you didn't let them go?'

'Of course I'm sure.'

'Then the person who let them all out was probably the murderer, wasn't he?'

'Never!' Mrs Collis said. 'He'd never have gone near those rats. He was as scared of them as I was. And that owl they were talking about – never! I know Stan Wall. He was queer about that sort of thing. When I wanted to keep a budgie, he said he'd leave if I did. Birds upset him, kind of, you know what I mean.'

'Stan Wall?' Susan said. 'But he couldn't have done it. The police said so.'

'They said he couldn't have killed Sandra, on account of his having only the one strong arm.' Mrs Collis put a cup of tea in front of Susan. 'Myself, I'm not sure about that. Like I said, he's ever so crafty. But if you want to know what they're saying in that pub down the road, where I went when those people in the cottage wouldn't open the door to me, they're saying it was Mr Riscoe killed Sandra, because everyone knew he'd been carrying on with her, like he carried on with every girl in the place. There wasn't one that was safe from him, they said. But Sandra was going to make trouble for him, they said, like telling Mrs Riscoe or something, so that's why he killed her. I can't tell you, of course, if any of it's true. But if it is, it could be why Stan would come back and kill Mr Riscoe. And he could've done that all right with his one strong arm, hitting Mr Riscoe with something on the side of the head. Stan's the man they've got to look for.'

She turned back to the dresser and poured out a cup of tea for herself.

As she did so, Nina caught Susan's eye, held it intently for a moment and with full intelligence flashing out suddenly through the blind look of shock, very faintly, warningly, shook her head.

11

Susan was beginning to have the feeling that what 'they' said in the pub in the village was a kind of Greek chorus to the tragedy developing at Bright's Farm. A hazy vision of all those anonymous faces, ranged in a row along the bar and spouting forth together their unanimous opinions, took a confusing hold on her imagination. They knew too much, they said too much, they seemed to matter too much. Without knowing them, she hated them.

But wasn't there generally a Messenger who told the members of the Greek chorus all that they really needed to know? Hadn't they a good deal of remarkably reliable information to go on? Somehow they always seemed to possess a very good grasp of the background of the main characters in the tragedy. But how could those people in the Dragon imagine for a moment that they knew anything about the Riscoes?

Such very strange people as the Riscoes . . .

Nina's strangeness now, as she signalled with that slight shake of the head that she knew that it was not Stan Wall who had killed Rob, perhaps even that she knew who had and that she was not going to betray him, gave Susan an extraordinary chill of fear for her. What would all those people in the Dragon make of it, those farmers and farm-labourers, stockbrokers, builders, lawyers, schoolmasters, who so enjoyed collecting daily in the bright little pub and pretending that they all liked and understood one another far better than they did?

Mrs Collis drank her tea, standing.

'All the same, what I can't make out,' she said, 'is why people like you and Mr Riscoe ever let that place to Stan. I can't see how he got round you to let him have it.'

Nina gave the smallest shrug of her shoulders, then sat immobile as before.

It occurred to Susan that this must be nearly the first time that she had seen Nina so still for more than a moment. She was nearly always on the move and in a hurry, running instead of walking and making those odd emphatic gestures with her hands. Even when she was busy writing the stories of Porky Pye and Croc-the-Dile, she scrawled her sentences as if she were inflicting wounds on the paper, kept jumping up from her chair, walking about, lighting cigarettes and stubbing them out and clawing at her shaggy brown hair. Susan had seen her at it.

'Yes, Nina, why did you let the cottage to him?' she asked.

'I don't know,' Nina said dully. 'We were just careless. We had a letter from him, saying he'd heard from his cousin in Swelsden that Mrs Gracie, her mother, was going to live with her and the cottage was going to be empty. The Gracies were the old couple who used to live there, you remember, till the old man died last year. The letter was quite pleasant, and we thought that as there'd been Gracies living in that cottage for fifty years, it would be the right sort of thing to do to let it to a nephew of theirs. And we didn't bother to check with the daughter. Crazy of us, of course. We keep doing crazy things.'

'You mean he wasn't related to the Gracies?' Susan asked.

'Of course not,' Nina said and Mrs Collis made a derisive noise, echoing her. 'We got suspicious almost as soon as he and the girl moved in, and a bit late in the day we asked the daughter in Swelsden about him. She'd never heard of him. But he paid his rent regularly and didn't do anything we could actually make a fuss about, and it's terribly difficult at any time to evict a tenant, so we let things ride.'

'But Rob did manage to get rid of him somehow.' Thinking of Conrad's story of the low-flying plane and the package falling in the field and Rob and Stan Wall meeting beside it, then going together to the cottage, Susan was watching Nina carefully as she spoke. Supposing that story was true, did Nina know anything about it?

There was no change of any kind on her face to suggest that she did.

'Yes, and then he let the place to Jocelyn,' she said. 'Jocelyn and Annette. . . .' At the last name something did alter in Nina's expression. Something flashed brilliantly for an instant in her black eyes as it had a moment ago, and then went out again. 'I'm so tired,' she added in a childish tone. 'I seem to have been tired for as long as I can remember. Just tired.'

Putting her arms on the table before her, she laid her head down on them, hiding her face.

Mrs Collis picked up the disregarded cup of tea, added more sugar and drank it herself. Then she briskly washed and dried the tea things and set them out again, saying that the gentlemen would be wanting tea too. Her air of possession of the kitchen was growing with every moment. She was refilling the kettle, while Nina still sat collapsed over the table, when Inspector Piggott came in, followed by Arthur, Fiona, Jocelyn and Conrad.

Inspector Piggott accepted tea from Mrs Collis, then began to ask Nina the same questions as Susan had just been asking her.

Arthur at once protested. Mrs Riscoe, he said, was in no fit state to talk. She needed a strong sedative and to be put to bed.

In this he was supported a few minutes later by the doctor who had been summoned to the studio to look at Rob's body. He was a scurrying little beetle of a man, who looked as if he were afraid that one of the inspector's large feet might crush him, yet in fact he asserted himself with sharp-voiced authority. The inspector did not argue with him, but as the doctor led Nina out of the kitchen, with Fiona in attendance, turned to Susan.

'I'm told you're quite well informed on the subject of falconry, Miss Lyne,' he said. 'If you don't mind, I'd like a few words with you.'

He gestured to the door, showing that he wanted to have those few words in private.

'But I'm not . . .' Susan began.

Arthur interrupted, 'She always says that, Inspector, about everything.' He smiled at her, touching her briefly on the shoulder. 'You're the nearest thing we've got to an expert, you know, with Nina out of action. So run along with him. It seems there are some very important questions to be asked.'

'But Jocelyn knows far more about falconry than I do,' Susan said.

'I've said all I can!' Jocelyn spoke with a startling violence which reminded Susan of the way that his hand had lashed out at the face of the woman in the cottage.

He seemed to feel himself that there was something wrong with his tone, for he made an obvious effort to relax his tight mouth and grey, stiffened features.

'You can help, Susan, please,' he said.

Wondering where Annette was and what sort of woman she could be not to have come here tonight, whatever Jocelyn had done to her, alternatively whether she had not been to the cottage at all and if it had been some other woman whom Jocelyn had struck in the bright, freshly painted room, Susan followed Inspector Piggott to the sitting-room.

The broken pane through which the brick had hurtled had not been mended and a current of air came in coolly through the opening. It seemed to Susan that there was a new dampness in the atmosphere, more than the mere dewiness of the night. It felt as if rain were coming to break the brilliant weather of the last few days.

Inspector Piggott thought so, too. Going to look at the broken window, where a few jagged shards of glass still remained in the frame, he remarked, 'If it turns wet and cold now, I suppose that python might pack up and die, if it isn't dead already.' He fingered a sharp fang of glass. 'Do you know how this happened, Miss Lyne?'

Susan told him briefly.

'But I thought it was falconry you wanted to talk about,' she said, 'not the python. I don't know anything about snakes, I really don't.'

He turned round to look at her, but his glance was as elusive as ever, darting away from her again to fasten upon an old white and gold Staffordshire spaniel on the mantelpiece. He crossed the room to it and caressed it gently with his forefinger. He seemed to find something supporting in the inanimate world.

127

That dog, smiling inanely back at him, would not drive him into disturbing moods of sympathy or condemnation.

'Yes, it's about the falconry,' he said. 'Let's sit down, shall we? There are only a few things I want to ask. I shan't keep you long.'

From habit, Susan sat down on the hearthrug. It was where she usually sat in that room. Inspector Piggott took a straight-backed chair. As if the sight of Susan in her tight jeans and loose jacket, squatting at his feet, with her tumbled hair hanging round her shoulders, made him suddenly realise how young she was, he smiled at her. He offered her a cigarette. When she shook her head, he said, 'Mind if I do?' Lighting one, he inhaled deeply.

'This falconry business now,' he said, 'this waking a falcon – that's the right term, is it?'

Susan nodded.

'Can you explain it to me a bit?' he said. 'Tell me just what Mr Riscoe was doing – would have done, I mean, if he hadn't been interrupted.'

Being interrupted, Susan thought, was a remarkable description of being murdered, rather like saying that a woman hadn't been interfered with if she had merely been murdered but not raped.

On the other hand, perhaps Inspector Piggott had meant just what he had said; meant that there had been some interruption, other than the murder, which had stopped Rob waking the falcon.

'Why, didn't he get started on it?' she asked.

'That's where I'm hoping you can help me.' But Inspector Piggott was looking again as if it were from the Staffordshire dog that he was expecting help. 'Did he or didn't he? Is there any way of telling?'

'Well, he made preparations to start,' Susan said. 'All those newspapers spread out on the floor round the chair, they were for the falcon's mutes – its droppings – while he kept it there through the night. Were there any there on the papers?'

'Droppings? Some.'

'If there were any there I should say Mr Riscoe must at least have started on the job.'

'And the job – tell me if I've got it right – was to sit there through the night with the bird on his arm.'

'Yes, talking to it and stroking it and keeping it awake, till he tired it into accepting him as a normal part of its life. Some falconers don't do it with the long-wings. Rob told me they just keep them hooded all the time. I expect it takes longer to man the bird – get it used to humans, you know – but of course it's much less exhausting.'

'Mr Riscoe, however, was meaning to make a night of it, was he?'

'Oh yes. Probably it's what the Emperor Frederick did, and what was good enough for the Emperor Frederick was good enough for Rob.'

'The Emperor Frederick?'

'Frederick the Second of Hohenstaufen, who was a Holy Roman Emperor in the thirteenth century. He wrote a thing called *De Arte Venandi cum Avibus*, which is supposed to be the greatest book ever written on falconry.'

'Well, well.' Inspector Piggott smiled a little. 'The thirteenth century – imagine that.'

Susan misinterpreted the smile. Examinations, written and oral, had been such a normal part of her life, she was so used to passing them with aplomb, that she did not realise that it was at this erudition coming from such a young and pretty girl that he was smiling; she thought that he was mocking Rob for his enthusiasms.

With some heat she said, 'Yes, why not? They knew a lot of things in the thirteenth century. And Rob loved the traditionalism of the whole thing. He loved to think he was doing what men did for more than a thousand years, until firearms came along. Rob hadn't any use for firearms. They spoiled all the joy and excitement of hunting for him. They took the whole challenge out of it. Besides, he said, with a gun you often just wounded a rabbit or a bird, but a falcon makes a very quick, clean kill.'

'I see.' The inspector's smile had gone. If he had ever felt any joy and excitement when faced by the dark challenges of his own life, he was not letting on about it. 'Now tell me just what

Mr Riscoe would have done when he was waking this falcon. He'd have sat there all night with the bird on his fist – his left fist?'

'Oh, he'd have got up and walked about a bit now and then, carrying the bird, and Mrs Riscoe would have taken him in some tea, I expect. But most of the night he'd have stayed in the chair.'

'With the bird always on his left fist, never the right?'

'So far as I know he always used his left. It's usually the left fist in Europe. It was something to do with court etiquette and keeping the sword-arm free. In the Middle East, though, I believe they use the right. But in Japan, where it all began, they use the left. Actually, I think Rob only had the one glove. It was there on the table.'

'I was coming to that. The glove was on the table and the standard lamp was close behind his chair, as it might have been if he were reading, or wanting for some reason to take a close look at something in a good light. Am I right, however, that if he'd been waking the falcon, he wouldn't have had the lamp so close to him?'

'Oh no, he'd have had it in a far corner of the room, so that the light was quite dim.'

Inspector Piggott took a thoughtful look at the fingernails of his own left hand, then flicked one of his rapid glances at Susan.

'Miss Lyne, I don't want to upset you, but you were in there, weren't you? You saw him dead. You know that he was killed by a violent blow on the left temple. Dr Murdoch says it looks to him as if it was done with something that had a bit of an edge to it, like a golf-club, say. We'll know something more definite about that later. Now I want you to think very carefully about what you saw. . . .'

Susan's face stiffened a little.

He went on quickly, 'We'll say for the moment that Mr Riscoe was interrupted after he'd started to wake the falcon. Someone he wasn't expecting walked in and insisted on talking to him. That might have upset the bird, I suppose.'

'Oh yes, an unmanned bird like that, she'd have bated wildly.'

'Bated?'

'Got nervous and furious, flapped her wings and dashed herself about and ended up hanging head downwards by the leash.'

'It sounds like what we used to say about the teachers – "Look out, he's in a bate." '

'It's the same word,' Susan said. 'It came from falconry in the first place.'

'Well, well. Conservative creatures, children. Still talking as they did in the thirteenth century, was it? It's the same with criminals. Plenty of their slang goes back to the Middle Ages. Not that they know that. Very modern, they think themselves nowadays. Now, as I was saying, suppose someone came into the studio and the bird got upset, might that have decided Mr Riscoe to put off this training business till another night?'

'I should think it might. He'd have been very angry about it, though.'

'Angry? I see – yet not distrustful.'

She put her head on one side, not following him.

He explained, 'He stopped this waking of the falcon, got up and took it out to that shed where he kept it, came back, dropped that leather glove of his on the table, moved the lamp up close behind the chair, sat down and let someone stand right in front of him, holding a weapon with which Mr Riscoe was just about to be killed. So it was someone he didn't distrust, wasn't it? And someone who was holding something that seemed normal to Mr Riscoe. He wouldn't have let someone like, say, Stan Wall, stand right over him with something out of character like a golf-club in his hand.'

'No, I see what you mean,' said Susan. 'But Stan Wall . . .'

'Yes?'

'He's got a withered right arm. And if Rob was killed by a blow on the left side of his head by somebody facing him . . .'

'Yes?' he said again and this time his gaze did not dart away when her eyes met his.

'That person was using his right arm.'

'Exactly.'

'So Stan Wall's out of it.'

'Again,' he said flatly.

131

'What d'you mean – *again*?' she asked. 'Do you think it was Wall in spite of his being left-handed?'

He gave a deprecating smile. 'Oh, you're much too fast for me, Miss Lyne. I haven't really done any thinking yet. Not what I'd seriously call thinking. But it's easier, you must admit, to see a man like Wall doing a couple of murders, with or without help from someone else, than to see, say, any of the people who are in the house at the moment doing them.'

He moved his weight slightly on the stiff-backed chair and Susan thought that somehow it was typical of him that he should have chosen to sit there stiffly all this time when he could just as easily have sat in one of the comfortable chairs in the room. It helped to keep his relationship with it impersonal.

'Now I think you've had just about enough for the present,' he added, 'so I won't go on and on asking you questions, but you'll go on thinking all these things over, won't you, and see if the circumstances in the studio suggest anything to you? A lot may depend on you.'

Susan nodded as she got up from the hearthrug. She went to the door. As she reached it, he stopped her with one more question.

'Just one thing, Miss Lyne. You needn't answer if you don't want to. Are you right or left-handed yourself?'

'Right, mostly,' she said. 'I'm rather ambidextrous really.'

'That's the trouble,' he said with a sigh. 'So are most people.'

She went out.

The feeling that there was something that he had not asked her was troubling her. Linked to it was a feeling that there was something that she knew and ought to have volunteered. Had it something to do with the story that Conrad had told her of Rob meeting Stan Wall, or Taylor, in the twilight field behind the cottage? No, because it was for Conrad to tell the inspector that, if it had ever happened.

This other thing was something that she knew of her own knowledge. It seemed to be on the tip of her tongue. Yet when she tried to take hold of it, to look at it, it slithered out of her grasp. Inspector Piggott had been right to stop question-ing her. What he wanted from her was some careful thought on an intricate subject, for which, as he had seen, she was far too tired.

It was some hours later, after a policewoman had arrived to take care of Nina, and Mrs Collis had been driven back to her hotel in a police car, and Susan had gone home with the Lasletts and was in bed, not sleeping and not quite awake either, that she suddenly realised what it was that she had failed to tell the inspector.

It was a very simple thing.

It was just the fact that there were three birds missing from Bright's Farm, an eagle owl, a goshawk and a peregrine falcon, and yet only two leashes had been left behind. One was the owl's, the other the goshawk's. Orlando and Celia were flying free. But Rosalind was almost certainly trailing her leash behind her, which meant that she had probably already got it entangled in the branches of a bush or tree, where she would hang by the feet until she died.

But just why did this point seem important? Inspector Piggott was unlikely to be much interested in the untimely death of a peregrine falcon.

The reason was, of course, that it might tell him something about Rob's last movements.

Sitting in his chair, absorbed in forming a relationship with the falcon, Rob would have had her jesses, the two leather straps that he would have fastened round her legs as soon as he obtained her and to which the leash would have been attached by the steel swivel, threaded between his fingers in the traditional way, while the leash hung down in a couple of loops, caught up by his little finger. That was the way in which falconers had been holding their birds through the centuries, a way that had been proved both convenient and secure, with almost no risk that if the bird, alarmed, suddenly bated off, the leash would be jerked out of the falconer's grasp and the bird escape.

Not if the falconer was alive. However, if he happened to be dead, the bird would soon work the leash free from his fingers and fly away to her own doom.

With wide-open eyes that ached from nervous exhaustion and from time to time spilled tears on to her pillow, Susan watched the dawn come, grey and cool, and heard the first bird calls and then their dawn clamour in the trees. She slept a little, woke, remembered that Rob was dead, for a while wept stormily, then slept again.

When she woke this time Fiona was standing by her bed with coffee and toast on a tray. Her face was drawn with strain and her eyes were red-veined with weariness. She was wearing a blue cotton house-dress and a cardigan.

'I looked in some time ago, but you were so sound asleep I didn't wake you,' she said. 'Now Mrs Whicker's started cleaning up downstairs, and doesn't want any of us in her way, so I brought this up to you.'

She put the tray down on Susan's knees.

'I didn't sleep at all,' Fiona went on. 'Not at all. I only went to bed for a short time, then I couldn't stand it and got up and went wandering about the house. And I saw a most extraordinary thing. A perfectly extraordinary thing.'

Her voice was so flat and empty that to someone who did not know her well it would have sounded as if she were commenting on some such thing as the change in the weather, but it told Susan that Fiona was in a state of extreme tension.

'What did you see?' Susan asked.

'I saw Jocelyn come out of the cottage – it must have been about five o'clock, I think – and drag something out to his car and bundle it inside. It wasn't easy. It was a long sort of package, long and heavy. And he drove off along the other lane – I mean, not the one to Bright's Farm but the one that joins the London road – and he came back about half an hour later. Isn't that strange?'

'Yes,' Susan said, 'it does sound strange.'

'At five in the morning, after all.'

'Perhaps he couldn't sleep either.'

'And there's another thing . . . they've found the weapon that killed Rob. And it's one of our garden hoes. One of *ours*! It and another one were in the ditch by our gate. Jim Burke found it there this morning.'

12

'But that's where we put them!' Susan sat bolt upright in bed. The tray nearly slipped from her knees. 'Conrad and I – we left them there when we decided to go into Swelsden for a coffee. I meant to put them away in the tool-shed when I got back. And then – with what happened – I forgot them.'

Fiona's eyes had widened. 'But whatever were you doing with them?'

'We took them when we went looking for Mrs Collis,' Susan said. 'Conrad lost her out there in the darkness and he was worried, so we thought we ought to look for her, and I was scared of the python, so we took the hoes with us.'

In the light of day what they had done sounded extraordinarily silly.

'I see,' Fiona said. 'In the circumstances it's distinctly a pity you didn't put them away.'

'I never thought of anyone taking them,' Susan defended herself.

'One of them. Only one of them.'

Susan gave a shiver. 'How do they know for sure it's the thing that killed Rob?'

'I suppose there are traces of his blood on it.'

'But I don't understand . . .'

'Thank God we don't have to understand!' Fiona said sharply. 'That's a job for the police. There've been enough of them around this morning. I don't think I can stand much more of it. I'm going into Swelsden to have my hair done. You'd better come too, I think. It'll help to get your mind off the horrible business and keep you out of the way of the reporters. We've had some of them around too.'

'I was going to say, I don't understand how anyone found the hoes out there in the darkness,' Susan said. 'I left them propped against the hedge beside the gate. They didn't show up at all.'

Fiona paused on her way to the door. 'That's an interesting point. How *did* anyone find them? You'd better mention it to the inspector. Now please don't be too long getting up. My appointment at the hairdresser is at eleven and I want to do a little shopping first, so I want to leave here in about half an hour.'

'I'm not sure I'll go,' Susan said. 'I was thinking—'

'You'd better come,' Fiona interrupted her. 'Your friend Conrad's been handling the reporters rather successfully so far. He got them away somehow. But if they see you, the girl who found the body and so on, and if you say anything about that hoe, they'll be after you like a pack of hounds – particularly when they see you're quite photogenic.'

Susan muttered unhappily. She had not the slightest wish to go into Swelsden to wander aimlessly about or to sit in a café to fill in the time while Fiona had her hair done. But she recognised the mood that Fiona was in this morning. She had passed the crisis of emotion when the tears streamed and her whole world seemed black and unbearable and without a ray of hope, and had reached the stage of apparently cold-hearted calm in which she looked so brisk, so competent, so detached from whatever disaster had overcome her that it was almost impossible to imagine that she had ever been upset by it. Yet this calm was only superficial. If anything troubled her, the whole process would repeat itself over again.

'All right, I'll be down as soon as I can,' Susan said as she put butter and marmalade on her toast and began to eat it.

She did not put on her jeans, shirt and straw sandals, but a green cotton dress, stockings and low-heeled black shoes. Brushing her hair back from her face, she fastened a wide black ribbon round it. Fiona, waiting for her in the hall and seeing her come downstairs, exclaimed: 'My, my, is this for the photographers?'

She herself had changed out of her house-dress into a cream shantung suit, with white gloves and a white handbag.

'I thought you'd prefer it if you had to be seen with me in Swelsden,' Susan said. Her reason for dressing soberly had been an only half-recognised feeling that there was something appropriate in doing this when a friend had died. 'You always complain about my clothes.'

'With reason.' But it was said with a smile and as Susan reached the foot of the stairs Fiona laid a hand on her shoulder.

'I'm just being foul, Susan. Don't take any notice of me. I'm in a tail-spin. I never was much good at coping with anything serious, was I? Arthur was in a foul mood too when he went off to the office and that's so unusual I wanted to sit down and start crying again. Come on, let's go. He went off in the Mini and left the Bentley for us.'

She opened the door and Susan followed her out in silence.

They were silent most of the way into Swelsden. The sky was clouded, the air chillier than it had been for several days and there had been a shower earlier. The road was shiny with moisture. Susan was glad of it. To see the people in the streets going about their normal affairs, unrocked by tragedy, was hard enough without having to see a blue sky over their heads and the glow of sunshine on their faces.

It was Fiona who broke the silence. 'I've been thinking about those hoes, Susan, and how anyone managed to see them there in the dark. Tell me something. How long after Arthur and I went up to bed did Conrad come and ring the bell?'

'I'm not sure. Twenty minutes or so, I should think,' Susan replied, 'only he didn't ring. I saw him outside and went out to meet him.'

'He didn't ring? Are you sure he didn't ring?'

'Absolutely sure.'

'Because someone did.'

Susan turned her head to look at Fiona, who seemed completely serene, as she always did when she was driving. She drove very well and loved it.

'Someone rang the bell after I'd gone out?' Susan asked.

'It must have been after you'd gone, if you didn't hear it,' Fiona said.

'And you didn't answer, because you thought it was Conrad.'

'You see, you'd said you'd go to the door if he came, and there was only one ring, so we thought that was what had happened.'

'Then you don't know who it was.'

'No.'

'But you think whoever it was saw the hoes there by the gate.'

'Don't you think that's how it must have happened? You said that someone just passing by wouldn't have noticed them.'

Susan tried to remember exactly how she had placed the hoes. She thought that she had propped them up side by side leaning against the edge, to the left of the gate. She was fairly sure that she had put them in a patch of deep shadow.

'So the question is,' she said, 'who could have come ringing your bell as late as that?'

'And I suppose the answer is, it might have been all sorts of people.' Fiona stopped the car as the lights ahead turned red. 'I've just been wondering though, if it mightn't have been Mrs Collis. You said Conrad lost her somewhere out there in the dark.'

'She told Nina and me later on she went to the Dragon to wait for the bus into town,' said Susan.

'Yes, Nina told me she'd said that. Nina said too that Mrs Collis told her the people in the Dragon had been saying that Rob had been having an affair with that girl, Sandra, and had probably killed her. Well, you saw the state Mrs Collis was in last night. Suppose she half-believed what she heard and because we'd been fairly nice to her earlier, thought she'd come in again and ask us what we thought about it. Then, when she'd rung, she lost her nerve and went away, and as she was going, saw the hoes and suddenly thought of going to confront Rob herself, and took one with her as a precaution . . .' The lights turned green again and Fiona drove on. 'I don't mean, of course, that I believe Rob did kill Sandra,' she said, 'or even was having any kind of affair with her. It's absurd to think so. But if Mrs Collis had walked in suddenly, waving the hoe, when he was waking the falcon, he'd have been in a blind fury and might have said or done almost anything. And that might just have convinced her he really had murdered her daughter and that she was in danger herself.'

'But if it wasn't Mrs Collis who rang the bell,' Susan said, 'who else could it have been?'

'All sorts of people, as I said. Jocelyn, perhaps. Nina, even.'

That silenced Susan. She had thought of both of those possibilities for herself, but she did not want to discuss either of them.

Annette was yet another possibility, Susan thought, if it had been Annette whom she had seen in the cottage with Jocelyn. If Annette had fled from him to the nearest house, rung the bell, then changed her mind about seeking refuge there with comparative strangers, seen the hoes at the gate, armed herself with one of them . . .

Yes, but why then go straight to Bright's Farm and murder Rob? Jocelyn, perhaps, but why Rob?

Susan began to chew one of her knuckles, frowning heavily. It would make faintly better sense if the thin figure in the cottage unrecognisable in coat and headscarf, had been Nina. Nina, who had torn up Annette's portrait, was said to have some dubious relationship with Jocelyn, and might have God knew what reasons for hating Rob. All the same, *Nina*, who had always been such a friendly, grateful person to work for, had written all those rather ridiculous yet always gay and charming books for children, had seemed to have her own odd kind of understanding of other people and patience with their tiresomeness . . .

Fiona's hairdresser was a Frenchman, recently imported to run the very pink and plastic hairdressing *salon* on the top floor of one of Swelsden's bigger department stores. When she had found parking-space a mere two hundred yards from the main entrance of the shop and she and Susan were walking towards it, she suggested that Susan should see if she could have her hair done too. But Susan was not in the mood for it. She said that she would wander about for a time, perhaps buy some shoes, or a blouse, or something, and end up in the coffee-bar in the basement, where Fiona could join her.

As Fiona presently was borne upwards in the lift, Susan began her wandering about. She did not really want to buy anything, but she loitered among Dress Materials, where the sweeping draperies of silks and velvets attracted her briefly. Then she moved on into Books and Stationery, where a display of the adventures of Porky Pye and Croc-the-Dile happened to be on show and made her want to do something shocking in the way of bursting into tears in public. Then she went into China and Glassware, where the hideousness of almost everything on view, reflecting what was presumably Swelsden taste, appalled her so much that it renewed her strength. Then she wandered into Lampshades, the ultimate nightmare.

After it Floor Coverings were almost a pleasure. She was just moving on once more, after standing looking for a moment at some plain broadloom carpeting in a rather pleasing soft cinnamon shade, which she had been pretending to herself she might order for her bed-sitting-room in London, when she came face to face with Jocelyn.

He smiled in his hesitant way and turned to look at the carpet over which she had had her not very absorbing day-dream.

'That's a pleasant colour,' he said.

His face was grey and his features had a pinched look which made his thin, high-bridged nose seem even more beak-like than usual. He was wearing one of his neat, dark suits which did not fit him very well and which brought out all the schoolmaster in him, totally disguising the man who had a successful play running in London. In spite of his smile, Susan had a feeling that he had been dismayed at seeing her.

She felt more tongue-tied with him than she ever had before.

'Are you buying a carpet?' she asked and at once she wished that she had not come up with something quite so stupid. It was hardly likely that the day after his brother's murder, Jocelyn would be buying a carpet.

He answered, 'Yes, I am, as a matter of fact. And I rather like that colour. But it's probably costlier than what I had in mind. I just want something for the bathroom floor. That bathroom in the cottage feels like a submarine cave. I thought a carpet would make it a bit less comfortless.'

'Yes,' Susan said. She could not think of anything more to say.

'I thought some of that rubber-backed stuff that I could lay myself would be about the best thing,' Jocelyn said. 'What do you think?'

She could only think of the extraordinariness of his being there, buying a carpet for his bathroom, when his brother was lying dead in some refrigerated locker in a police mortuary, or perhaps, at this very moment, having the fearful indignity of a *post mortem* inflicted on his helpless body.

'I thought you laid some linoleum in the bathroom when you moved in,' she said.

He appeared to think that the shocked protest in her voice was at his extravagance.

'It's perfectly awful old stuff,' he said. 'When I looked at it today, it struck me it added the final touch of squalor to the place. Even the bare boards, with all their splinters, were better. Then I thought the pleasantest thing would be to have a carpet. I've got the walls painted white and with something in a nice cheerful colour on the floor, it won't look so bad.'

'Was that Annette's idea?' Susan asked. 'Did she send you out to buy it?'

'Annette? She hasn't been here,' Jocelyn said. 'In fact, I don't believe she's ever been inside the cottage. She saw it from the outside, of course, when the old Gracies lived there, but that's all.' He looked vaguely round the big silent department. 'I wonder how one discovers someone who might like to sell one something.'

Susan gestured at an immobile, elderly man in a corner whose austere expression suggested that he did not want his meditations disturbed by people who could not possibly have any intentions of buying anything; people who, if he noticed their existence, would certainly tell him that they were 'just having a look round'.

'Try advancing on him in a slightly threatening manner,' Susan said, 'and tell him very precisely what you want, and when he tells you he can't recommend such stuff and that what you want is something at twice the price, you explain you weren't asking for his recommendation. I'm quoting Fiona, though, as a matter of fact, she always ends up buying the most expensive thing in sight.'

She was talking too much now and it still sounded absurd. She turned to go.

Jocelyn took her by the arm. 'Don't go. Come and help me choose something. Then come and have some coffee. I want to talk to you. Please.'

141

There was anguish in his voice, and his face, as he turned it to her, was so full of misery that she was horrified all over again at her stupidity. Of course he had only come out to buy the carpet because he had not been able to bear staying in that awful empty little cottage any longer. He had had to go out and do something. Anything.

Fiona, with some of the same feeling in her, had come out to have her hair done. Jocelyn had come to buy something for his desolate home, even though he would probably never live in it now.

Susan stayed and helped him to make up his mind that some very cheap carpet in an apricot shade was what he wanted.

The assistant said he supposed that the gentleman would want it delivered and what were the name and address, please.

Jocelyn said thank you, but he would take it with him.

This resulted in a very long delay, while the carpet was rolled into a bulky parcel, but at last, with Jocelyn hauling the parcel awkwardly along, he and Susan made their way down to the coffee-bar in the basement, where Susan had promised to wait for Fiona.

Nearly ten minutes later it was still not clear to Susan what Jocelyn had wanted to talk to her about when he had asked her to stay with him. He had sat silently beside her all that time on a bench against the wall, had occasionally sipped his coffee, fiddled with the spoon in the saucer, and gazed vacantly into the middle of the room. Susan could not make up her mind whether or not she ought to try to make him talk to her. She found it felt almost impossible to talk.

Her first hostility to him had melted, and now it was the intensity of the pain in him that overwhelmed her, making her almost shrink from him – pain, she thought, because of what had happened between him and Annette; as much as because of Rob's death. Was that why she winced so when she tried to speak?

But suddenly she knew what she had to do.

'Jocelyn, I've got to tell you something,' she said. 'Do you realise that everything you do in that sitting-room of yours can be seen from Arthur's and Fiona's house? I saw some-

142

thing last night you probably don't know I saw. I looked out of my bedroom window and I simply saw it. You ought to know.'

He turned his head to look at her and she was horrified for an instant to see what looked like blind terror in his eyes. Then he closed them and when he opened them again they were expressionless. His mouth smiled faintly.

'Go on,' he said mildly. 'What did you see?'

'I saw you in there with a woman,' she said. 'I thought it was Annette, and I saw you knock her down.'

'Ah,' he said.

'Anyway, that's what I think I saw,' she said. 'What it looked like.'

'It wasn't Annette,' he said. 'She didn't come.'

'She didn't?' She had not felt sure till that moment that the woman had been Annette, but now she was convinced that it had been and that Jocelyn was lying.

He lied, if that was the truth of it, very calmly. 'She telephoned yesterday after lunch. I was still at the farm. She said she'd read about that girl's murder in the papers and wouldn't it be better if she didn't come – kept clear of it, you know, for the sake of the school and those children she's taking abroad? I said, yes, of course.'

'Then who . . . ? '

He gave his gentle smile. 'You know, Susan dear, I don't think that's any of your business. But it wasn't anything important. I can swear that most solemnly, if it'll set your mind at rest. It was a piece of – well, play-acting.'

'Literally play-acting, do you mean? Something to do with that play you're writing?'

'I'm not writing anything at the moment, I'm just trying to shape up a few ideas. No, I meant it was just a meaningless show of temper on my part. Perhaps you didn't know I've got a temper. The truth is, I've a fairly fiendish one, which may not show itself for months at a time, but when it does I'm capable of behaving like a five-year-old child. It's not nice. Afterwards I'm always disgustingly sick and go in for an orgy of apologies and self-abasement. A depressing story, isn't it? I'm glad you've never seen that side of me. But you needn't worry, there's no real violence in it.'

'But it *was* Annette in there with you,' Susan said.

For a moment she thought that she was going to see that temper of his. There was a dark blaze in his eyes, his mouth became lipless. It gave him the look of having a staring death-mask for a face.

She went on, 'You needn't worry, Jocelyn, I won't tell anyone about it. I understand you'd want her to keep clear of everything to do with the murder.'

'Which murder?' he asked.

'Sandra's, of course, Rob's happened later, quite a bit later than that. I expect Annette had gone already.'

'It wasn't Annette you saw.'

'Oh, Jocelyn—' She said it with all the affection that she could, to show him that she was back on his side.

He leant sideways to whisper into her ear, '*It – was – not – Annette!*'

She could feel his breath warm on her face as he hissed the words at her.

'Will you stop meddling in what doesn't concern you, child?' he went on. 'I don't want it. I don't need it. I'm grateful to you for telling me that what goes on in the cottage is so visible from outside. It was quite brave of you to do it. None of us likes to admit we've seen things we weren't meant to see. Thank you for it. And the first thing I'll do when I get home is hang up curtains of some sort. But now can we please talk about something else?'

'What?'

'Anything. You. That dress you're wearing. It's charming, it suits you. What made you suddenly decide to dress like a woman?'

When she was silent, he went on, 'I'll tell you. You're begin-ning to stop feeling overshadowed by Fiona. She's always eleg-ant, she's always feminine and flawless to look at. And she's always been there, older than you and cut to a more common-place pattern than you, which the young think means being more secure and better liked than their own odd sort of selves can ever be. Naturally you were always horribly afraid of trying

144

to compete with her. So you asserted yourself by being different at any price. But now at last something has made you begin to see not merely that you're always going to have to go on being different from her, but that that's not in itself a bad thing, and so there's no need for you to go on making a fuss about it. Hence the nice dress. I hope you've some more of them.'

He was talking, Susan realised, about the first thing he had thought of that might lead her mind away from Annette.

She leant her head back against the wall behind her, feeling bleakly rebuffed, but managing, after a moment, to respond obligingly, 'Fiona isn't commonplace, you know. Sometimes I think she's a lot crazier inside than I am, or she used to be till she met Arthur. And it wasn't her looks or her femininity that used to impress me so, it was her courage. She'd dare anything. Things I'd try to copy, feeling miserable with fear. She'd do them as if she didn't give them a thought. I don't think she did either. She'd ride anything and climb anywhere and go out with anyone and tell our poor father the most awful lies about it all without even a twinge of discomfort. And she adored him, that was the odd thing, just as she adores Arthur. Only I think Arthur must understand her a lot better than my father ever did. Arthur isn't commonplace either, you know. I used to think he was, because of that army look he has and his stodgy way of talking. But I think now three quarters of that is shyness or something. He's really very . . .' She fumbled for the right words. 'Acute. Observant. Understanding.'

'A pleasant thing to discover in a relation,' Jocelyn said rather drily.

'Yes.' She finished her coffee. 'I don't suppose you like your relations any more than Rob did. I wonder what was really so wrong with them.'

'It doesn't matter any more, does it?' he said. 'There aren't any left that count.'

'Did Rob count?'

'He was the only one who did. And he counted so much, I wanted to be just like him, as you wanted to be like Fiona, when the only way to find out just how much I cared for him was to learn how completely different I was . . .'

145

He looked up as a shadow fell across their table.

It was Fiona. Her hair, unattractively rigid under a coating of lacquer, was set in a style that did not suit her very well, but she had had the relaxing, purging experience of an expensive hair-do and was obviously feeling the better for it.

She shook her head when Jocelyn, standing up, suggested that she should join them.

'No, Susan and I must be getting home,' she said, 'but I'm so glad I ran into you, Jocelyn. There was something I was coming over to ask you. I don't expect you think any more than I do that Nina ought to be left alone at the farm, so I wanted to ask if you'd be moving in with her, or shall I go and ask her to come and stay with us? Which do you think would be best?'

Jocelyn seemed confused, taken quite unprepared by her question.

'I hadn't thought of moving there,' he said. 'But you're quite right, she oughtn't to be alone. If you could have her . . . But there are the animals, of course. She'd never leave them.'

'There aren't many left,' Fiona said. 'Only Touchie and Oliver, and she could bring them with her.'

'That's awfully good of you,' Jocelyn said, still in that muddled-sounding way. 'It seems a lot to ask of you, though. Perhaps I ought to go . . . Only there are one or two things . . .'

Such as an old village scandal, Susan thought, which might not have a shred of truth in it, but might easily be revived at a time like this to do both him and Nina damage.

Fiona seemed to have thought of this too, for she said that she was sure that the best thing would be for Nina to come to stay with her and Arthur and that she would drive straight to Bright's Farm now to fix it up.

The three of them left the coffee-bar together, Jocelyn clasping his unwieldy parcel to him like a drunk friend whom he was seeing safely home.

At the entrance to the store they separated, to go in different directions to their parked cars.

'Whatever was that thing he was carrying?' Fiona asked when he was out of earshot.

'A carpet,' Susan said.

'A *carpet*?'

'Yes.'

'What was he doing, buying a carpet – I mean, on a day like this?'

'He may have wondered what you were doing, having your hair done.'

'That's different. That's definitely quite, quite different,' Fiona said. 'Having my hair done is a thing I always do when there's trouble.'

'Your normal behaviour pattern?'

'What? Oh well, you can put it like that if you want to. But I don't see buying a carpet as part of anyone's normal behaviour pattern. Did Jocelyn say what he wanted it for?'

'The bathroom.'

'The *bathroom*?' Fiona stood still to give Susan a shocked look before unlocking the Bentley. 'Wait!' she exclaimed, as if her own snugly carpeted, pale grey and yellow bathroom were not one of the first cares of her life. 'I ask you . . . !'

13

They drove to Bright's Farm. But Nina declined Fiona's invitation. It wouldn't be a case of bringing only Touchie and Oliver with her, she said, but a tribe of chickens and three geese, and that would be too much to ask even of the Lasletts.

Fiona suggested that Nina could bring the monkey and the dog and go home to the farm as often as the chickens and the geese required to be cared for. But Nina still shook her head. Susan thought that she would probably have refused to move even if there had been no poultry to serve as an excuse for staying on in her home.

There had been a change in Nina, which Susan could not define. It was a mystifying kind of reposefulness. Many of the lines in Nina's vivid face had disappeared, which turned it into an oddly youthful and innocent-looking mask. Susan thought that all Nina wanted for the moment, now that the police had gone and the old house had settled creakily into its normal quiet, was to be left alone to come to terms with what had happened to her.

Yet when, very tentatively, Susan suggested that she might move in there for a few days if it would help at all to have her around, Nina's eyes swam with tears and she said, 'Oh, Susan, would you?' She seemed quite unreasonably moved. 'Fiona, would you mind? Just for a day or two. I'm so used to having Susan around, it wouldn't feel so – strange. You wouldn't mind?'

'Of course not, it's an excellent idea,' Fiona said. 'I've just been worrying at the thought of you here by yourself. If I were in your shoes I know I couldn't stand it for an hour. I'd have been in some hotel by now if someone hadn't come in to help.'

'You're so sweet, both of you,' Nina said with her strange, new tranquillity, yet with deep emotion.

Embarrassed by the intensity, Susan said hurriedly, 'I could be getting on with the typing. I could keep out of your way unless you wanted me.'

Nina nodded and smiled.

Fiona and Susan drove home, having arranged to bring Susan back with her belongings after lunch.

'She's still in a state of shock, you know,' Fiona said. 'I hope you realise what you may be in for. She may break down completely presently.'

'Then she really ought not to be alone, ought she?' Susan said. 'I didn't do the wrong thing, did I, offering to stay?'

'Oh no, no, quite the best thing possible. I'm glad you suggested it. And if anything happens you can't cope with, get in touch with us at once. In any case, we'll ring up or look in later.'

But Nina did not break down. Her strange calm persisted. After a time Susan began to think that it was not shock at all, but that some deep internal change had already taken place in Nina. Something in her, a wound-up spring that had always kept her in continuous motion, running, gesticulating, chattering and exclaiming, had gone slack. Something had run down and stopped. And she seemed to be finding the experience not altogether unpleasant.

She said nothing of this herself and perhaps did not even know that it had happened. When Susan, who thought that perhaps it might be her own presence that was inhibiting a normal show of grief, suggested that she should go to the study and type, Nina said, 'Oh, don't bother about that now. Who knows if I'll ever want to send the book off now? Poor old Porky, I've got quite fond of him after my fashion, but I suppose this is the end of him. It was Rob's illustrations that sold the books. No, stay and talk to me, Susan. Talk to me.'

And she really seemed to mean it. For a time she wanted Susan to talk. She did not want to talk herself. The flood of speech that so often poured out of her, drowning any attempts made by her hearer to get an occasional word in edgewise, had dried up. She took Susan into the sitting-room, lay down on the sofa with

Touchie cradled in her arms and, fixing her big grey eyes on Susan's face, repeated gently, 'Oh, do talk, Susan.'

Immediately Susan's mind became a blank, but at last, after thinking desperately, she said, 'You don't really think the Porky stories will stop, do you?'

'Oh, I should think so,' Nina answered.

'You could send this one off anyway, then give yourself time to think,' Susan said. 'You may find you want to go on with them later.'

'On the other hand, perhaps it would be nice to write something quite different,' Nina said. 'I shan't have to worry about money, you know. Not for some time. With Swelsden spreading out as it is, the value of this place has gone up enormously since we bought it. I'll get thousands more for it than we gave.'

'Then are you going to sell it and move away?'

'Oh yes. You can't see me living here by myself, can you?'

'I suppose not.'

'And I shan't be missed. Rob and I didn't manage to get ourselves liked in the neighbourhood. Think of those Merrow children. Heaving a brick at that window there.'

'That didn't mean anything. It was mostly mischief. They might have done it to anybody.' Someone, Susan noticed, had made a neat job of removing the remaining splinters of glass from the window-frame and pasted a sheet of plastic over the opening. She noticed too that the plastic was stippled with raindrops. The shower that had been threatened since the morning had come. 'Arthur and Fiona will miss you, anyway,' she said.

'A little perhaps, but it'll be Rob they really miss, not me. People always liked Rob better than me. And d'you know why? It was because he didn't give a damn for any of them. He was always just himself. And so few people are just themselves, it's incredibly attractive to them when they encounter it. I haven't been my real self for I don't know how long. Perhaps I haven't any real self. But God, how I loved Rob, Susan. How he went on attracting me in spite of everything!'

Susan wanted to ask inquisitively, 'In spite of what?' but said nothing.

After a moment Nina answered the question without its having been asked. 'For instance, the animals. Did you ever notice they're all named out of *As You Like It*? I sometimes said to myself, "Yes, Rob, my darling, it's As *You* Like It," – this life we live. I don't mean I minded it. I dare say I've really been happier than most people. But sometimes I used to think, here we are, we could write our books anywhere, we're still fairly young, we could be travelling, seeing, learning all sorts of things . . .' The words were beginning to flow out of her, but they were quiet and thoughtful, as if she were speaking of things that had happened long ago. 'Then there were always the women, of course. That made me sick at first. I haven't much self-confidence, I can't stand much rivalry. I thought I'd have to walk out. Then I began to realise there was nothing in it. They fell for him – even Fiona did for a little while, did you know that? – and he played along for a time out of – oh, almost a sort of good nature. No, it was really the Celias and Rosalinds I had to compete with. And the obvious way to deal with that was to join in. "If you can't beat it, join it." That was simple.' She smiled. 'But then Annette came along.'

'Annette?'

At the astonishment on Susan's face, Nina laughed a little. 'God, yes, didn't you know? . . . Oh, you haven't met her, have you? I was forgetting that.'

'Annette and Rob were in love with each other?'

'She was in love with him and she wouldn't believe she couldn't get him. She so nearly did, you see. That was some years ago. It broke up her engagement to Jocelyn and nearly smashed our marriage, and there were some terrible rows between Rob and Jocelyn. Before that they'd been unusually close to one another, with Jocelyn rather hero-worshipping Rob and Rob thinking that Jocelyn had all the real brilliance he hadn't quite got himself. And somehow, in a rather wonderful way, they weren't jealous of one another about it. Annette destroyed all that, then slipped out of sight. Then she and Jocelyn met by chance last year and it looked as if the whole miserable story was going to start all over again. They got more or less engaged, he brought her here—'

'But why?' Susan broke in. 'I don't understand. If all this had happened, why on earth did he bring her here, of all places?'

'Because he isn't entirely a fool. He knew he'd got to find out if she'd really got Rob out of her system or not.'

'And she hadn't?'

'No, oh no!'

Susan was out of her depth. Trying to take in what Nina, in this calm way, was telling her about her marriage, she felt as if she were floundering in waters that had suddenly turned out to be dark and bottomless, where she had always assumed that there were only safe and sunny shallows.

'What happened?' she asked.

Again a smile flitted across Nina's face. 'She hadn't got Rob out of her system, but Rob had just got Celia into his. He was training her, d'you remember? And Rob with a new hawk hasn't room in his mind for anything else. It was quite funny to watch. Annette tried terribly hard to take an interest in Celia, but it happens that she's frightened of birds. She doesn't even like to touch them or be in the same room with them. So Jocelyn and I just sat back and waited. Another funny thing . . .' Nina smiled broadly at the funniness this time. 'I heard we created quite a scandal in the village. We'd be seen driving about together, and having drinks together. Fiona told me the worst was believed. But all we were doing was trying to keep each other's spirits up till the inevitable happened – what we both thought was inevitable when we weren't feeling discouraged. And at last it did. Rob told Annette she was being a flaming nuisance, always upsetting his precious hawk, and she got into a rage and departed.'

'What did Jocelyn do then?'

'Stayed on here, very sensibly. And met you.'

'Oh.'

'I used to wish you'd fall in love with each other, you know. But I suppose at your age he seemed about a hundred years old.'

Susan dropped her eyes to avoid Nina's contemplative gaze. 'Just about,' she muttered. 'Yes, just about a hundred.'

'And that, I thought, was that,' Nina went on. 'Rob and Jocelyn seemed back to normal with one another, and Jocelyn's play was

152

put on and was a success, and he seemed quite happy – as happy as someone like him ever can be. And when Rob told me he'd managed to persuade the Taylors to move out of the cottage and was thinking of asking Jocelyn if he'd like it, because we both thought he ought to take the plunge and get out of teaching, I thought it was a very good idea. I was entirely in favour of it. And then, like a bolt from the blue, Jocelyn wrote that he'd married Annette and that she'd be coming here, too.'

The slight colour that had seeped back into Nina's cheeks while she was talking suddenly drained away. All her tranquillity left her. She sat up so abruptly that Touchie, startled, went leaping out of her arms to the top of the bookcase.

'You don't know what it did to me, Susan! I'd thought all that was over, that I was finished with her, that horrible, horrible woman. I did some crazy things. I didn't always mean to. I mean, I wouldn't intend to break something Rob was particularly fond of, but I'd do it – things like that. I let the python get away. It was because I was horribly frightened about the future, so I was trying to take a kind of revenge on him. And then one evening – you'll probably hardly believe it – I quite deliberately tore one of his drawings to pieces. It's the only time I've even thought of doing such a thing. I loved his work, I loved it as a part of him. But there was this drawing of Annette in his studio and I couldn't bear seeing it day after day, so I pulled it down and tore it into little bits and stamped on them. And then at last he understood what was happening to me and instead of going into one of his black moods, which could make me feel suicidal, he was sweeter and more loving than he'd been for a long time . . . I've been so happy the last few days, Susan. I've felt Annette really didn't matter any more and couldn't do us any more harm.'

She smiled again as if she were still quite happy and lay back comfortably on the sofa.

'But I don't understand,' Susan said stupidly. 'I simply don't understand. I don't understand why Jocelyn—'

'Why he accepted the cottage? Why he brought her here again?'

'It just seems mad to me.'

'Oh, I don't know. It's just possible, isn't it, that she did get Rob finally out of her system last year? It's pretty insulting to a woman, particularly one who's so used to being beautiful, to find she rates a good deal lower than a goshawk. But there may have been other reasons. I thought of several. One was that she married Jocelyn at last just because of the cottage, because it would bring her near Rob. There's madness for you all right – in me, I mean.'

'There'd be madness in her, too, if it was truth.'

'Oh, she isn't mad at all. She's rather stupid and very spoiled, but not in the least mad.'

'What makes Jocelyn love her so?'

'Oh, God, what makes anyone love anyone? Her beauty, and the way she tramples on him – he likes that – and the feeling that for once he fought Rob to the end and won. He wouldn't have wanted it once, but she made him like that . . .' She stopped, listening. 'There's someone outside. Who is it?'

Susan went to the window, which was sheeted now with heavily falling rain.

'Police,' she said.

Inspector Piggott, turning his collar up against the rain, was just getting out of a car.

Nina gave a long sigh. 'I've been expecting them back all day. Will you let them in? But Susan—'

Susan paused.

'Don't leave me alone with them unless they insist on speaking with me privately. There was a very senior man of some sort here this morning. I felt he thought I'd killed Rob. So I'd feel better with you around.'

Susan nodded and went out to the door.

Inspector Piggott was alone and said nothing about wanting to speak to Nina privately. He peeled off his raincoat, draped it over a chair in the hall and followed Susan into the sitting-room. Nina made a show of starting to get up from the sofa, but the inspector made a gesture to stop her and took a chair facing her, all with only a few muttered words of polite greeting.

Then abruptly he asked, 'Mrs Riscoe, did you know your husband was engaged in smuggling?'

154

It brought Nina bolt upright on the sofa again. Her eyes blazed. 'He was not!'

'You think he wasn't?' The inspector's gaze had already found the china dog on the mantelpiece and fixed itself there with weary detachment.

'I know he wasn't,' Nina said.

'Then you know something about the smuggling, do you, to be so sure he wasn't involved in it?'

Nina's look became confused and she sank back on the cushions.

'I don't even know what you're talking about,' she said. 'And I suspect you oughtn't to have asked me a question like that without warning me first.'

'It's just that Stanley Wall – the man you knew as Taylor – was arrested this morning in Dublin,' he said, 'and he's confessed to being a member of a small organisation that's smuggled a variety of goods into this country. He's named the others in the group and he claims your husband was one of them.'

Nina stared at him in silence. He seemed to find this more unnerving than angry speech would have been, for his gaze on the china dog became as glacial as if the thing had tried to bite him.

'The last lot of stuff to be smuggled in,' he went on, 'was a consignment of watches, worth several thousand pounds. Wall took them to London when he left here and disposed of them to the usual purchaser. Then he appears to have heard of the death of the girl, Sandra, got in a panic and made off for Ireland, where, as I said, he was taken in for questioning this morning, and has been talking ever since to clear himself of the charge of the two murders. And he appears to be clear of both of them. With his withered arm he couldn't have strangled the girl, and his alibi for last night is absolutely watertight. He was in Dublin already when your husband was killed. But he's accused Mr Riscoe of being a member of the gang of smugglers. He says that's why he let him have the cottage. The open space behind it was a good place for dropping the goods from a low-flying plane. But later they decided between them it was time for Wall to move away, because one night they were seen out there by young Ives, of the *Swelsden Weekly Advertiser*. And that part of the story's corroborated by Ives. Last night, before I'd heard any of this, he told me about having seen a plane drop a package in the field behind the cottage and your husband and Wall go out and pick it up and go back to the cottage together.'

'Inspector,' Susan said. She had remained standing, with her elbows propped on the high back of a chair. 'Those watches . . .'

'Yes, Miss Lyne?'

'Wall had them with him in those suitcases I saw him put into the car on Thursday afternoon, hadn't he?'

'That's right.'

'Then that's why Sandra laughed and danced.'

'Danced?' he said. 'Ah yes, I remember your mentioning that.'

'I thought it was because she was so glad to be going to London, or because she was glad to have got rid of Wall,' said Susan. 'But of course it was because he'd got clear away with all those watches right under the nose of the police. Just think, he was actually putting his cases into the car when Mr Burke appeared. Think of what Stan and Sandra must have felt. And then all Mr Burke wanted was to know if they'd seen a ten foot python. No wonder she went wild with laughter.'

The china dog seemed to be restored to favour, for he smiled at it. 'I shouldn't wonder if you're right.'

Nina's voice cut in jerkily, 'Inspector, isn't there something about Wall you haven't told me yet? Hasn't he accused Rob of the murder of Sandra?'

He seemed reluctant to answer, uncertain whether or not he should. Stirring uneasily on his chair, he said after a moment, 'Yes, he made that accusation. But there's no evidence at the moment to support it.'

'Is there any against it?'

'I hoped perhaps you could give me some, Mrs Riscoe.'

'Then you haven't already made up your mind Rob did it.'

'Of course not.'

'But you have decided to believe this smuggling story.'

Again he took his time to reply. 'Will you tell me why I shouldn't?'

She made some of her swift, mysterious passes in the air with one hand, as if she were about to produce truth, like the ace of hearts, suddenly out of her sleeve. 'Because he wouldn't have bothered,' she said. 'He wouldn't have been interested.'

He answered mildly, 'There's always money.'

'It may seem strange to you, but we had as much as we needed,' she said. 'I don't mean we didn't always *want* more – of course we did – but we didn't *need* it.'

'You're sure?'

'What? Oh, I see what you mean. Had Rob any financial needs I wasn't supposed to know about? The answer is, no. I'm not afraid to say it. No. If he became at all involved with another woman, he never bothered to conceal it. If he needed money for anything unexpected, I knew all about it. His one real vice, if that's what you can call it, were his birds, and that doesn't come so very expensive. For a long time now, we've been earning more than enough for the way we wanted to live.'

He asked again, 'You're sure?'

Nina turned to Susan. 'Don't you agree with me? Smuggling, taking risks with the law, getting involved with people like Wall, wouldn't have had any attraction whatever for Rob.'

Susan thought it over and said, 'No, I don't think it would.'

'You don't seem quite certain, Miss Lyne,' Inspector Piggott said.

'Oh, I'm quite certain,' she said. 'But I was wondering . . . Have you any theory yet about why the birds and the rats and mice were let loose?'

'I can only think it was an act of utter hatred against Mr Riscoe, something like going on emptying all the bullets in a revolver into a man when the first shot's killed him. Or else it was simply to create confusion.'

'Do you mean to conceal something else?'

He stood up quickly. It was just as if Susan, like a tactless hostess, had given him a heavy-handed hint that he had overstayed his welcome.

'Yes, well, one has to try to think of everything,' he said. 'But it's all guesswork so far. There's nothing definite to take hold of. Thank you for answering my questions, Mrs Riscoe. I'm sorry to

157

have taken up so much of your time. You and Miss Lyne have been very helpful.'

In a flurry of polite phrases, he made for the door.

Susan went after him and tried to challenge him again, but he only murmured something about Mrs Riscoe holding up wonderfully, went out through the heavily falling rain to his car and drove away.

Irritated, because she was more profoundly perturbed than she understood, Susan closed the door behind him.

An instant later she opened it again because she thought that she heard the car returning. But it was not the car, it was Conrad's motor bike. Conrad's head, in his crash-helmet, was lowered to shield his face from the rain, he was encased in waterproof leggings, gloves and jacket, and looked like something that might just have arrived from outer space.

Propping up the bicycle, he came towards the open door, peeling off his gloves.

'I came to tell you,' he said with unusual sombreness, 'I believe I've found the falcon and it's dead. It's up in a tree by the road, hanging by its leash. I thought you might want to come and take a look at it.'

14

Susan looked at the pouring rain. It had already made broad puddles on the drive. She thought what a good thing it was that someone had put that sheet of plastic over the broken pane in the sitting-room window. Perhaps one of the policemen who had had to stay about the farmhouse for most of the night had filled in a few spare moments of boredom by showing off his skill as a handyman.

'Well?' Conrad said.

The raindrops, striking the puddles, made them look as if they were being raked by machine-gun fire. Not that Susan had ever seen machine-gun fire, except in films. But there was a sharp edge to the cloud that was disgorging the rain and beyond it the yellow gleam of sunshine.

'Suppose we wait a few minutes,' she said. 'This'll soon be over. And I'm not sure that I ought to leave Nina.'

Nina heard their voices. She came to the door of the sitting-room.

'What's happened?' she asked.

'Conrad thinks he's found Rosalind,' Susan told her. 'She's got the leash entangled in the branches of a tree and she's dead.'

'Where?' Nina asked.

'A little way down the lane,' said Conrad.

'How did you find her? Did you go looking for her?'

'As a matter of fact, I did,' he answered. 'From the little I know of falconry, I thought she couldn't have got far in woods like these, trailing a leash, and I thought it might be important to find her. So I strolled around, searching, and heard her bells tinkling and there she was.'

'I didn't know you knew anything at all about falconry,' Susan said.

'Well, I don't, to speak of, but I've read some books about it – and don't say you didn't know I could read,' he said.

'I wish you'd go and get her if you can,' Nina said. 'This rain's going to stop in a minute.'

It had begun to stop already as she spoke. Its sharp, hissing sound was muted. The drops that still struck the puddles fell into them with soft little plops. In another moment the rain had gone. A rainbow shone in the sky.

Susan and Conrad started down the lane. Under the trees it still felt as if it were raining, for there was enough breeze to keep the leaves shivering, shedding their moisture. Conrad took Susan almost to the corner where the lanes divided. Then he turned off along a path, or perhaps it was only a chance division in the brambles and elderberries, which led them into a glade surrounded by tall beeches. The massive tree-trunks were grey-green with lichen. Overhead the branches interlaced so densely that only a greenish twilight penetrated the leaves. The sunlight above made them gleam like a roof of opaque green glass.

Susan had just time to think that this must have been the way that the dead body of the girl Sandra had been brought from the cottage, that she must have been dragged through this quiet place to be hidden deeper in the wood, when Conrad stood still and pointed upwards.

From one of the branches above them, at the end of a leash, dangled a brownish, bedraggled object. A faint, eerie little sound of tinkling bells came down to them as the dead bird twisted gently in the breeze.

'Yes, it's Rosalind,' Susan said.

'It's going to be a bit difficult to get her down,' Conrad said. 'Do you think you could stand on my shoulders and reach that branch?'

Susan looked at the distance and looked at Conrad.

'No, I could not,' she said, 'you couldn't stand my weight.'

'Why do you always need so much convincing that I *can* do quite a lot of things?' he demanded. 'Actually, I'm beginning to wonder if it isn't a sign of growing affection. There are a lot of people who never trust the people they love most, even to do the simplest things, like turning off the gas when they go out, or remembering to cash a cheque before the bank closes – my mother's like that with my stepfather and they've been very happily married for fifteen years. But she'll unthinkingly trust life and limb to any perfect stranger who happens along.'

'The simple fact now, all the same, is that we need a ladder,' Susan said. 'There's one at the farm, a good long one.'

'All right, let's go and fetch it.'

They turned back to the opening in the brambles.

But someone, just then, was coming along the path towards them. They heard quick footsteps, and Jocelyn thrust his way through the wet bushes into the glade. Tugging to free himself of a long trailer of bramble that clung thornily to his jacket, he looked up as the bells overhead tinkled faintly.

'I saw you come in,' he said. 'I thought this might be what you were after.'

'I thought she must be somewhere close,' Conrad said.

'Yes, it would have been incredible luck if she'd got clean away.' Jocelyn considered the distance from the ground to the branch from which the bird swung and made the suggestion to Conrad that he had made to Susan. 'I believe if you could manage to get on to my shoulders, you might just be able to reach her – anyway, if you'd a stick or something to poke the leash loose with. Want to try it?'

'All right.'

'Let's look for a stick.'

They hunted among the bushes till they found one, a long, not too brittle branch of elder with a fork at one end, that must have been torn off a tree in one of the winter storms.

The scene that followed would have made Susan want to laugh if she had not felt that what the two men were trying to do was to be deadly serious in its consequences. Conrad was agile enough to climb on to Jocelyn's shoulders and Jocelyn was more muscular than his slender build suggested; however, neither of them had been in the habit recently of doing this kind of thing and they made two or three false starts, which resulted in both of them falling over in the soft leaf-mould and becoming very

161

irritable with one another because the other was not more adept at his part of the job.

But at last Conrad managed to climb on to Jocelyn's shoulders and while Jocelyn swore to himself in a muttering tone and grew red in the face with straining, poked gingerly with the stick at the leash entangled in the twigs till the dead falcon fell almost soundlessly to the ground.

Susan picked her up by the leash, a strangely shrunken bundle of sodden feathers, the brownish feathers of the immature bird, not the slate-grey and whitish buff that she would have had a year later. As she hung limply, head downwards, from the leash attached to her jesses, it was hard to imagine the strength that there had been in the beating of her wings, the deadly power of her talons.

Conrad jumped down from Jocelyn's shoulders and Jocelyn stretched, gave a slight groan and began to massage his shoulders.

'I'll take her along to Nina,' he said. 'I was going to see her anyway and she may want to know what happened.'

He took the falcon from Susan and walked off through the bushes.

The sound of his footsteps had faded before either Susan or Conrad spoke. They had remained where they were, both looking aimless as if suddenly they did not know what to do next. Getting the dead bird down from the tree had seemed to matter immensely, but what now?

'I'm beginning to wonder if we oughtn't to have left her up there in the tree and telephoned the police,' Conrad said. 'Never touch anything, that's the first rule when you find evidence.'

'Well, it's done now,' Susan said. 'I'm glad at least Celia and Orlando got away safely.'

'Will they survive on their own in the wild?' Conrad asked.

'For a time, anyway, I should think,' she replied, 'unless some fool of a farmer shoots them. There'll be a fine supply of white rats running around loose for Orlando, and Celia's a very competent killer. The trouble for both of them may be that they've learnt to trust us humans too far and won't be afraid when they see a gun pointing at them.'

'I suppose it was important to find Rosalind,' Conrad said. 'But what does it really signify, Susan, now that we have?'

'I think it means that Rob was waking her when he was killed, sitting there in the chair with her on his fist.'

'Why?'

'Because, if he'd been alive, he'd never have let her get away like that, with her leash attached to her, to a certain death.'

'But accidents happen.'

'I don't think that particular accident would have happened. He was far too experienced. As I see it . . .' Susan frowned in concentration, looked down and began to draw a sort of diagram in the soft ground with her toe. 'I think Rob was sitting there in the chair with Rosalind when the murderer came in. Rob might not have heard him, but Rosalind would have got alarmed at once and bated. Have you ever seen a falcon do that? Do you know what it would have been like? Rob would have had the leash and jesses wound round his left hand so that she couldn't have got away from him, and she'd have been jumping about and flapping her wings furiously, and they're pretty long, strong wings. While she was doing that, the murderer *could* have hit Rob on the left side of his head – but not if he was standing in front of him. Rosalind would have got in the way. So I think . . .' The diagram on the ground was beginning to look like a plan of the studio. 'I think that means Rob was killed by someone standing behind him, and since he was hit on the left side of the head, it suggests a left-handed murderer. But not Stan Wall. He was definitely in Dublin when Rob was killed.'

'But what about the lamp behind Riscoe's chair?' Conrad asked. 'That would have got in the way of someone who came on him from behind, just as much as the falcon would have if he'd stood in front.'

'The lamp could have been moved up afterwards, just to conceal the left-handedness of the killer, and Celia and Orlando and all the rats and mice could have been released for the same reason. It could have been done just to hide the fact that Rosalind got away with her leash attached to her only because Rob was dead already.'

163

'Wouldn't it have been cleverer of the murderer then to let Celia and Orlando go too with their leashes attached to them?'

'Yes, but perhaps he just couldn't make himself let them go like that. Rosalind may have got away with her leash because he was taken by surprise, but perhaps he simply couldn't send the others off to die like her.'

'It's a picture of a pretty rum murderer you're building up,' Conrad said. 'He doesn't mind killing a man sitting quietly in a chair, but he can't bear to be responsible for the death of an owl and a goshawk.'

'Well, how else could it have happened?' she asked.

'I don't know. I know animal-lovers can be pretty peculiar people, but still that doesn't seem to make sense.'

All of a sudden, without any premonition of it whatever, Susan began to cry. Tears poured from her eyes, her body began to shake. Her voice went high as she tried to go on talking in spite of the racking sobs.

'Such a lot's happened since last night, Conrad, and none of it makes sense! Yet it happened. There was that thing we saw through the cottage window. Then Jocelyn said Annette never came here at all. I don't believe him. I'm sure she was the woman we saw. But he's hiding it. And last night – no, this morning about five o'clock, Fiona said, she saw Jocelyn come out of the cottage with a long parcel. She said it looked heavy and difficult to manage and he put it into his car and drove away and came back about half an hour later. And then, when she and I were in Swelsden this morning – she was having her hair done and I was wandering about, filling in time – I met Jocelyn buying a carpet to put down in his bathroom. That's what he said. A carpet for his bathroom. He thought the linoleum he'd put down made it look even more squalid than the bare boards. Rob was dead, Nina was all alone at the farmhouse and Jocelyn was in Swelsden, buying a carpet for his bathroom!'

Conrad put his arms round her.

Still crying as hard as ever, Susan hid her face on his shoulder. As he was still wearing his oilskin, it felt a little like being embraced by a beetle, yet there was astonishing comfort in it. It dawned on her as a remarkably original thought that there were times when people of your own age seemed to understand you far better than anyone else.

'Of course, I see what you're really afraid of,' he said. 'You're afraid Jocelyn Riscoe killed his brother and his wife. For reasons I suppose I can guess. And all that confusing stuff about letting the animals go – he's probably so used to them that he'd have let the hawk and the owl go without their leashes as a matter of course, without thinking out what a blunder he was making. And when he'd killed his wife, he cut her body up in the bathroom and made a parcel of her and drove away and dumped her somewhere, and then when he came back he found he'd stained the bathroom floor, so this morning he drove into Swelsden to buy a carpet to hide the stains—'

'Conrad!' She slapped him hard and sprang away from him, clapping her hands over her ears. 'Stop it! I won't listen! It couldn't have been like that.'

'He's left-handed, of course?'

'No, no, no!' she shrieked at him.

'Isn't he? Are you sure he isn't?'

'I'm sure! He isn't!'

'Then perhaps it's his wife who is.'

'Annette?' Susan's voice broke as she said the name and it came out as a hoarse whisper.

'Yes,' Conrad said, 'suppose it was she who killed Rob Riscoe and came back and told Jocelyn what she'd done and that's when he struck her and killed her.'

'But you said yourself she told you through the door she was all right,' Susan said.

'Yes, well, perhaps Jocelyn came back into the room a minute or two later with a knife or something and finished the job off properly. Then he thought that if he wanted to get away with having murdered his wife he'd better conceal the fact that she'd murdered his brother – in fact, that she'd ever been near the place at all. So he went and faked all that stuff with the lamp, removing the glove from his brother's hand and letting the birds go and all, to make people think the murder was done from in front by a right-handed person, after his brother had given up trying to wake the falcon that night. Then, in the early morning, when he thought no one was watching him, he disposed of Annette's body and went and bought the carpet—'

'Stop!' Susan screamed at him again. 'It wasn't like that. It can't have been like that. Jocelyn couldn't kill anybody.'

'That's something I wouldn't say of my nearest and dearest, let alone myself,' Conrad said. 'But if you feel so strongly about it, it seems to me there's just one thing for us to do at the moment.'

'What's that?'

'A little snooping.'

'You're always snooping.'

'There are times when it's not only justifiable but entirely necessary. It is now. Come along. We're going to look round the cottage while Jocelyn's along at the house with Nina.'

'How do you think you're going to get in?'

He pushed back his oilskin, felt inside the pocket of his jacket and brought out a key.

'It's the one you gave me the other day to give back to Nina. I clean forgot it.'

He took her by the arm and pushed her towards the opening in the bushes.

She resisted the thrust of his arm. 'I'm not going with you.'

'Why not? He'll never know. Besides, it'll be far better for you to come too, because if I simply tell you what I find, you'll never believe me. You never believe anything I say.'

She saw the point of that and weakened. Though she felt as if she were doing something really evil in the way of spying, were committing one of those sins of distrust against someone dearly loved for which there could be no forgiveness, there was no energy left in her hanging back as Conrad hauled her along the path through the brambles.

But she half hoped to see Jocelyn returning along the road from Bright's Farm so that the plan of going secretly into his cottage would have to be abandoned. But the lane was empty. There was no one to see what she and Conrad did, no one to stop them. He opened the cottage gate and with his hand still on her arm, as if he were afraid that she might suddenly run away and leave him to take all the blame if he were caught, hurried her up the path,

166

unlocked the cottage door and pushed her ahead of him into the little room.

He had once said to her that anything could happen there, absolutely anything, and that that was what the cottage was for, that it was there simply to be a setting, a background for some strange and dramatic event. Susan had jeered at him, asking what could a cottage be for except for people to live in. Since then a dramatic event had happened there, the murder of the girl Sandra, and who knew what else, and the thought of this, acting on Susan's horribly guilty feeling at being there at all in this secret way, made the atmosphere of the place almost more than she could bear.

Yet the room was far pleasanter than when she had seen it last. The furniture that had been under the dust-sheet was now in place. There were some shabby but comfortable-looking armchairs, a bookcase, a gate-leg table, a dark red cord carpet, round the edges of which the floor had been freshly stained. The strong smell of the stain, mingling with the smells of paint and distemper, produced an odour that would be rather overpowering to live with, but was not in the least sinister.

Jocelyn had not yet hung up any curtains, but apparently he had taken seriously Susan's warning of how visible everything was that happened in this room, and had hunted out some old blue velvet ones from among the furnishings that had arrived from his mother-in-law's home in Scotland. They were hanging over the back of a chair, immensely thick and heavy and lined with dark blue sateen. Once they were up, they would screen the room as effectively as a wartime black-out.

But they were far too long for the little cottage windows and Jocelyn had already started to shorten one of them. Started, but stopped in the middle, and no wonder, because to judge by the unevenness of the cutting, the little snips and jags, the tool that he had tried to use on the two thicknesses of material was the small pair of curved nail-scissors that lay on the window-sill, beside a screwdriver and bradawl, which he must have used to put up new curtain rails.

Yet there was a large and practical-looking workbasket open on the table. It was the workbasket of a woman who took her sewing seriously and in which there was certain to be a pair of good-sized scissors. Puzzled, Susan looked into it. There were no scissors there. There was everything else. There were pins, needles, a thimble, a tape-measure, buttons, hooks-and-eyes, reels of cotton, tape, elastic, but no scissors.

Pondering this, having completely forgotten for the moment that it was the carpet for the bathroom floor that she and Conrad had come to investigate, she heard him call her, 'Come and take a look at this, Susan. What do you make of it?'

She went to the sitting-room door and into the primitive little kitchen, out of which the bathroom opened. Only yesterday morning she had done the washing-up here for Jocelyn. Only yesterday. It felt half a lifetime ago. So far as she could see, nothing more had been done in the kitchen since she had stopped working there, except that a little unwashed crockery had accumulated in the sink. Yet something, as she looked around, nagged her mind. What was it?

Yesterday, besides china and glass, she had washed up a good deal of silver, solid old stuff that had probably come from the home of Annette's mother, and some aluminium cooking pots, and other kitchen utensils, wooden spoons, ladles, strainers, a fish-slice, an apple-corer, a potato-peeler . . .

'What are you doing?' Conrad asked. He had come to the door of the bathroom and was looking at Susan curiously as she stood in the middle of the kitchen. 'I want to show you . . .'

She did not hear him. Suddenly she had moved towards the little kitchen cabinet that had been placed next to the old stove. There were two drawers in the cabinet above the cupboards. She pulled the drawers out and with hands clumsy from nervousness, rummaged amongst the wooden spoons and all the other odds and ends that she had put there yesterday. When she could not find what she was looking for, she started to take everything out. She thought that the thing might actually be there, staring her in the face, and that she was simply too wrought up to see it.

Conrad came up beside her. 'What are you looking for?'

She let her hands fall to her sides. 'There's no potato-peeler.'

'Then give them one as a wedding-present – though some people actually prefer a knife for peeling potatoes. I do myself.'

168

'No, you don't understand. There was one here yesterday. I washed it up and put it in one of these drawers. I know I did. I *know* I did, Conrad.' She spoke as if he had been trying to argue with her. 'And there aren't any scissors either in Annette's work-basket. Don't you see? She *is* left-handed, just as we were saying. And Jocelyn's been getting rid of all the evidence that she is, the left-handed cutting-out scissors, the left-handed potato-peeler. I wonder if he's got rid of her golf-clubs, too. They'd be left-handed, wouldn't they? They were in that corner there yesterday, with those mops and brooms and they're not there now!'

Conrad caught her by the arm as she flung it out to point. 'Just a minute. I want you to look at what I've found in here. I think it's probably just as important as the scissors and potato-peeler.'

He pulled her forcefully into the bathroom.

It had become a very different place from what it had been a day or two ago. The bath was still rust-streaked, but it was clean. The walls were white. Jocelyn must have worked on them for most of the night. The curtain of cobwebs was gone from the window. Also the badly pitted linoleum which Jocelyn had laid before he had thought of buying carpet to cover the floor was gone. The splintery boards were exposed. The carpet itself, still in the parcel in which he had brought it from the shop, was standing in one corner.

'Well,' Susan said, looking round, 'what's so important?'

'He's got rid of the linoleum, too,' Conrad said.

'Well?' she repeated.

'He could have left it as an under-lay for the carpet, if it hadn't been necessary for some reason, like stains, say, to get rid of it along with whatever was in that parcel your sister saw him shifting this morning.'

'No!' Susan said violently.

'What's happened to the linoleum, then?'

'I don't know.'

'You did say you saw it here, didn't you?'

'Yes, I did.'

'Then what's become of it?'

'I don't know. It could be anywhere. You haven't looked around, have you? You haven't looked upstairs, or outside, or anywhere. And I do know this. Jocelyn couldn't kill anybody. If he's got rid of the linoleum, it's in some way to protect Annette, like getting rid of the scissors and the potato-peeler and the golf-clubs . . . Golf-clubs!' Her voice rose sharply. 'That's it, of course! The linoleum was pitted all over by someone who'd walked about in golf-shoes – in shoes with metal studs. That's why it looked so awful. So when Jocelyn got rid of the golf-clubs, he got rid of the linoleum too. That's what was in that long parcel – the linoleum and the golf-clubs—'

'All right, all right,' Conrad interrupted her. 'But there's something else peculiar in this bathroom. Come and take a look at it.'

He bent, pointing at the floor. There was a row of screws there, holding down six planks that had been sawn through just inside the door. About five feet further into the bathroom, another row of screws had been driven into the same six planks.

'What does it mean?' Susan asked.

'I don't know,' Conrad said.

'It's probably just something to do with the plumbing or the electric wiring.'

'Probably. All the same, I think we want a screwdriver. Wait a minute, I've got one in my tool-kit.'

'There's one in the sitting-room, on the window-sill,' she said.

'Fine.' He fetched the screwdriver and in another moment was on his knees in the bathroom, working at the screws that held the six planks down to the joists under the floor.

He and Susan were both so concentrated on what he was doing that neither of them heard the light steps approaching the cottage, or even the slight creak of the front door as it was opened. Conrad found it quite easy to remove the screws. Though they and the screwholes were old, the screws had obviously been taken out recently and replaced carelessly. He had them out in a heap and was preparing to lever up the first board when Jocelyn, white-faced with fury, leapt at them from the kitchen, elbowing Susan out of his way, seizing Conrad by the shoulder and pulling him backwards.

'What the hell do you two think you're doing?' Jocelyn yelled at them. There was a wildness in his eyes that Susan had never seen before. His face-muscles were working and he seemed to be

170

trying to go on shouting at them, but the sheer violence of his anger almost dried the words up in his throat. 'What are you doing?' It was to Susan that he was speaking now. 'Always snooping, watching, spying . . . Why the hell d'you do it? What do you want? What are you trying to do to me?'

'I wasn't . . . I only . . .'

Susan could never have finished what she started to say, even if there had been no interruption, because she did not know what she was saying and had nothing to say.

But there was an interruption, a shout from Conrad. 'Look out!'

When Jocelyn had turned on Susan, Conrad had stooped swiftly for the screwdriver that he had dropped and he had just levered up two of the sawn-through planks in the bathroom floor.

An instant before he shouted something below had stirred. It had stirred sluggishly, like a slow ripple moving across the mud on the surface of a dark, soft bog. Then it heaved and writhed. Then while the three of them stood petrified in the bathroom doorway, a ten foot length of angry python came sliding up at them out of the hole.

15

None of them moved. Not one of them could have moved. Perhaps this was fortunate, for the snake, after a swift little darting movement of its head to left and right, shot between Jocelyn and Conrad and out through the door. The speed of its sliding motion over the floor was incredible. It went straight across the kitchen and into the sitting-room, making for the open door, for sunlight and air.

Someone shrieked. It was Nina. She was standing in the middle of the sitting-room when the snake appeared and she screamed with all her might.

Immediately afterwards there were two shots.

Susan did not realise at first that that was what they were, because there was hardly any bang, but just a sort of whine. Yet there was a dreadful kind of decisiveness in the sound that left her frightened and disbelieving. It was Arthur who had fired and killed the snake. He and Fiona had just come to the door of the cottage as the creature slithered into view and he had fired past Nina and shot it in the head.

As Susan, Jocelyn and Conrad, all rather dazed, jostled each other to get from the bathroom to the sitting-room, the dappled length of the python went still on the red cord carpet.

Arthur strolled forward and gave the snake a tentative jab with his shoe. The smell of explosive was strong in the little room. He looked down at the small pistol in his hand.

'And Fiona's been laughing at me for carrying this thing,' he said. 'I thought myself I was probably a bit crazy. Still, I'm not sorry I stuck to it.'

Nina did not thank him.

'Poor Adam, I don't suppose he'd have done us any harm,' she said. 'Rob swore he'd be quite friendly so long as he wasn't frightened.'

'My dear Nina, I didn't feel in the least inclined to find out if he was frightened or not,' Arthur said. 'I was frightened myself and that was quite enough for me. You can have his skin made into some very handsome shoes and handbags.'

Jocelyn was looking at the gun. 'How long have you been carrying that thing, Arthur?'

'Ever since the girl was killed,' Arthur answered. 'And don't ask me if I've got a permit for it. I haven't. I picked it up in Germany just after the war and it's been at the bottom of a trunk for the last twenty years. I'd almost forgotten I had it. But knowing there was a killer loose in the neighbourhood made me think of it suddenly, so I dug it out.'

'You seem able to handle it pretty well still,' Jocelyn said.

'Instinctive. If I'd stopped to think what I was doing I'd probably have shot Nina slap in the back.' Arthur turned to Nina. 'Sorry, my dear, it was mad of me to risk it. Jocelyn, you don't happen to have a drink in the place, do you? I'm beginning to feel the need of one.'

If he did, it was mostly from elation at having slain the serpent, Susan thought. She was beginning to understand how Arthur thrived on excitement.

Fiona, on this occasion, was not thriving on it. She looked white and shaken. She put an arm round Nina and said, 'Did he scare you to death?'

'Arthur?' Nina gave a laugh. 'The snake did. Startled me out of my wits, anyway. I think I'm past being really frightened for the moment. Even the policeman who thought I'd murdered Rob didn't frighten me.' She strolled across the room to the fireplace and stood looking intently at the photograph of Annette on the mantelpiece. 'The fatal woman,' she remarked. 'Unseen, unheard, yet present all the time. Now if she'd been murdered, there'd be nothing stupid about suspecting me.'

'No one suspects you of anything,' Jocelyn said. 'You shouldn't talk like that.'

'Yet I suspect everyone of everything, isn't that odd?' There

173

was something unnerving about the continuing placidity with which Nina spoke. 'My head's been full of horrid thoughts for a long time, d'you know that? I've had horrid thoughts about you all, when you probably thought I liked you. And I did like you most of the time. But so often you looked at me as if I were just that odd sort of woman you had to put up with if you wanted to have Rob around, and when I saw that I hated you. This woman—' She picked up the framed photograph of Annette and with abrupt violence dashed it down on the hearth. The glass, shattering on the stone, made almost as much noise as the two shots. 'She was the worst of you all. If she ever comes to live here, I warn you, Jocelyn, I'll kill her!'

He stooped and picked up the photograph and stood looking down at it.

'Don't worry,' he said gently. 'She won't come here. She'll never come here now.'

Suddenly Nina began to cry. Wailing like a child, she threw herself down in a chair, crying with screaming sobs and her fists pressed into her eyes. Her body trembled all over.

'Oh, Jocelyn, I'm sorry, I didn't mean to do that!'

'It doesn't matter.' He put a hand on her jerking shoulder, then looked round at the others. 'What are you all doing here? As I remember it, I left this place locked.'

'I had a key,' Conrad said. 'The Taylors left it behind. I meant to give it to Mrs Riscoe and forgot.'

'So, because you had a key, you came in,' Jocelyn said. 'As an explanation, it seems a bit inadequate, but at a time like this, I suppose, it may as well stand.'

'I wanted to look at your bathroom floor,' Conrad said. 'I heard you'd been seen getting rid of a mysterious parcel at crack of dawn this morning and then that you'd been into Swelsden to buy a carpet for your bathroom floor. I thought I'd like to look at the floor.'

'You did? And I'm supposed to understand why?'

'I came in with him,' Susan blurted out.

Conrad seemed to feel no shame at what he had said, but her cheeks turned scarlet.

'And we saw them letting themselves in in rather a furtive sort

174

of way,' Fiona said, 'and thought we ought to come over to see what was up. Then of course we saw you and Nina come in, so we thought we'd look in anyway and see if you'd all come over to us for drinks.'

'Drinks – ah yes,' Jocelyn said absently. 'Arthur wanted a drink, didn't he?' He opened a cupboard, took out an unopened bottle of whisky and handed it to Arthur. 'Help yourself. Now let me get this straight . . .' He sat down on the arm of a chair, lit a cigarette and looked at Susan, whose face turned a deeper red, then looked back at Conrad. 'A parcel got rid of at dawn and a carpet for my bathroom – how does that add up to a necessity for you to look at the bathroom floor?'

'Frankly,' Conrad said, 'I thought you might have murdered your wife last night, dismembered her body in the bathroom and got stains on the linoleum. So then, I thought, you'd made up a parcel of them and driven off with them to dump them some-where. But then you'd have realised that if anyone knew you'd laid that linoleum yourself in the last day or two, as Susan did, it was going to look a bit odd to them if you simply took it up again without putting something else down instead, so you bought the carpet—'

'Conrad!' Nina had come abruptly out of her crying fit and was sitting up, her eyes shining wildly behind the swimming tears. 'Are you quite mad?'

'I shouldn't be surprised, or at least if I come to it some day,' Conrad answered. 'But you know, Mr Riscoe, Susan and I did see your wife in here with you last night. We did see you strike her and saw her fall down. So I'm not just making it all up as I go along.'

'I told Susan, it wasn't Annette,' Jocelyn said in a level voice.

'Oh, come now, who else could it have been?' Conrad asked.

'I simply can't follow all this,' Arthur said. 'It's the first I've heard of Annette being here. And all this talk about the bath-room floor – I can't remember when I last heard such fantastic-sounding nonsense. What I'd like to know is where this snake came from. Can anyone tell me that?'

'It came out of a hole in the bathroom floor,' Jocelyn answered.

'No, seriously, I want to know,' Arthur said with a sudden, new harshness. 'Where did it come from?'

'Out of a hole in the bathroom floor,' Jocelyn repeated. 'Let's go and look at the hole, shall we? I was too scared when the snake came out to do much thinking about how the poor creature got in there.'

He led the way out to the bathroom.

It was too small for them all to crowd into it together. One by one they filed in after Jocelyn, took a look at the hole in the floor and returned to the sitting-room. The hole, in size and shape, was not unlike a small coffin. It was about five foot long, two foot wide and eighteen inches deep. But its sides were of brick, not of wood, with a metal ventilator at one end to keep it dry.

'The smugglers' cache,' Jocelyn said. 'The place where Stan Wall put that consignment of watches you saw him bring in, Ives. Nina's been telling me about all that. I suppose he built the thing himself when he moved in. A nice bit of work, clean and dry and convenient.'

'But that doesn't affect the question of what happened to your wife last night, does it?' Conrad said. 'Or what was in the parcel you got rid of this morning?'

'No, perhaps it doesn't. She wasn't in the parcel, however,' Jocelyn said. 'She isn't dead. And if you doubt me, ring up that damned school she works at and ask them if she isn't there at this moment, busy organising a tour of Rome for some groups of little nitwits from the Sixth Form.' He reached for the bottle of whisky, which Arthur had put down on the table, unopened. 'Now let's all have that drink. Glasses, please, Susan. You'll know where you put them.'

She went out to the kitchen to fetch them, hearing Jocelyn continue, 'Really, Ives, why not ring them up if it'll set your mind at rest? You'll find Annette's alive, safe, well and all in one piece. There's no telephone here, but you could ring up from the farm or from the Lasletts' house. Why not go and do it?'

'Because I don't want to miss that drink,' Conrad replied, 'and on the whole I'm ready to accept your word, Mr Riscoe. About that, I mean. But that your wife wasn't here – I'm sorry, no. I saw her. And she's a left-handed woman, and it was a left-handed person who killed your brother.'

'No.'

Susan returned to the sitting-room with a tray of glasses.

'She *is* left-handed, Jocelyn,' she said. 'That's why you got rid of the linoleum, not because of bloodstains. It was pitted all over with the marks her golf-shoes must have made when it was down on some floor in her old home – which is where I suppose you were when the golf ball came through the window and it felt like being shot at. Do you remember telling me about that? And you didn't want anyone to see the marks and start thinking about Annette being a golfer and finding that she'd got left-handed golf-clubs. So you got rid of them this morning, with the linoleum and her cutting-out scissors and the potato-peeler.'

'Yes, that's right, she *is* left-handed!' Fiona exclaimed. 'I remember now I played golf with her once last year. I noticed it then.'

'No!' Jocelyn said, more violently than before. 'All right, she was here for a short time yesterday and she may be left-handed. But she didn't kill Rob – or Sandra. Aren't you forgetting Sandra in all this? Annette can easily prove she was miles away when Sandra was killed.'

Arthur took the tray of glasses from Susan and began pouring out the drinks.

'Why should we take for granted they were killed by the same person?' he asked. 'What did Annette do while she was here, Jocelyn? Mightn't it help all round if you told us that? Knowing the amount we do it's impossible not to suspect her.' He put a glass of whisky into Jocelyn's hand. 'The truth might clear the air.'

'What hope is there that you'll believe the truth?'

Jocelyn took another long look at the photograph of Annette, which he had been holding all this time. Then he put it face downwards on the table. The gesture, for some reason, made Susan think of a woman having her head muffled in a blanket, then being hustled out of sight into a waiting van by a group of policemen. An unrecognisable, faceless woman. You often saw that sort of scene on television.

Arthur was handing the other glasses round.

'Why not try us and see?' he suggested.

'All right,' Jocelyn said. 'It was like this. Annette arrived at

177

Swelsden on the four-ten train, as she'd said she would. I went to meet her. She hadn't heard anything about Sandra's murder. I told her on the drive back here. She went very silent for a time and I said if she didn't like the idea of staying here, we could spend the night at a hotel in Swelsden, or I could put her on the next train back to London, if she'd prefer that. She just shook her head and said the situation had better be faced straight away. We got here . . .'

He began to pace about the little room.

'We came in and she said at once that she was feeling ill and wanted to lie down. I thought it was the feeling of being here in this cottage where the girl was killed and I offered to take her to a hotel in Swelsden again, but she said no, she'd be all right presently and she went upstairs and I got on with some painting.

'I'm not sure when I realised she'd left the house. I remember thinking it was time to start scratching together a meal of some sort, then getting the feeling that the house was empty – I don't know if you know what I mean – and I went upstairs and found she wasn't there. She'd obviously lain down for a time and then slipped out very quietly.' He stood still and gave a dazed look round. 'I seem to be telling you everything, much more than there's any point in telling.'

'Go on,' Arthur said quietly.

'But it almost sounds – the way I'm telling it – as if I think she's guilty.'

Susan thought that this was the first time, while he was telling this story, that Jocelyn fully recognised the strength of his own belief in Annette's guilt.

'Go on,' Arthur repeated.

'Well, it was only a little while after I discovered she'd gone that she came back,' Jocelyn said. 'She was in a state of complete hysteria. She said she'd been to the farm to try to see Nina and that Rob was dead. I couldn't take it in at first. I tried to get out of her why she'd wanted to see Nina and she told me it was to tell her that everything was over between her and Rob and she needn't be afraid there'd be any trouble because we'd come to live here. Something happened to me then – I can't explain it – I

178

suddenly felt absolutely sure that the reason Annette had come, why she'd at last agreed to marry me – was just to be near Rob. I went half out of my mind and I started hitting her. She fell down. That brought me to my senses and I stopped. She said again that Rob was dead in the studio and I ought to go and see for myself.'

'She didn't come to see me,' Nina said. 'I haven't seen her at all.'

'No, because just as she got to the studio she saw you come out,' Jocelyn said. 'She said you seemed to look straight at her and didn't see her, and there was blood all over your blouse. You walked back to the house as if you were in a trance, leaving the door of the studio open behind you. Annette went there and looked in and saw Rob, dead.'

Nina frowned as if she were trying to see something through a wavering fog.

'Yes, there *was* blood on my blouse,' she said, 'and I couldn't stand the feeling of it and I changed it. I just dropped it on the floor and left it there. I couldn't bear to touch it again and the police have it now. I think that's partly why that Chief Superintendent, or whatever he is, suspects me. But after I did that I can't remember anything until I heard that woman screaming – Mrs Collis. I remember thinking for a moment I was doing the screaming myself, then I realised it was coming from outside, and I went out to see what was happening. You know, I think I'd almost forgotten about Rob being dead. When I saw him again it felt more like seeing something I'd known was going to happen than something I'd already seen.'

'Well, Annette found Rob dead and she thought you'd killed him because of her,' Jocelyn said. 'She came straight back to me —'

'What about the rats?' Arthur interrupted. 'Were they loose then?'

'No, I set them loose,' Jocelyn replied.

'Good God, why?' Arthur asked.

'Because almost the first thing I realised when I got there was that Rob had been killed by a left-handed person,' Jocelyn said. 'You see, he was sitting there with the left side of his head smashed in and the glove was on his hand and the lamp was in

179

the corner, so that the light in the room was very dim, and the falcon was gone. I made sure that the falcon was gone by going out to look in the shed, just in case he'd put her back there. But of course he hadn't. So that meant he'd still been waking her when he was killed. You see, it would have been very difficult to hit the left side of his head from in front of him while that great creature was flapping about in a frenzy on his left hand, so he must have been hit from behind, that's how I worked it out, before he'd had time to turn round to find out who was there. And the bird escaped after he was dead, trailing the leash behind her and of course got tangled up almost at once in the trees and died there. So I started letting the other birds loose, and the rats and mice.'

'I still don't get it,' Arthur said. 'Why?'

'Well, Annette's left-handed. You've realised that for yourselves, or I shouldn't be telling you this. And I didn't know – I don't know – of any other left-handed person around except Stan Wall, and for all I knew, he was miles away.'

'He was,' Conrad said. 'He was in Dublin.'

'So I set about deliberately changing things around to make it look as if the murderer was right-handed,' Jocelyn went on. 'The first thing was to make it look as if Rob had stopped waking the falcon. I moved the lamp back to its usual place behind his chair. I took the glove off his hand and put it down on the table. Then I let all the animals loose. I thought it would look as if it had been done by the murderer in sheer spite, and that Rosalind had been let loose with the others. But of course I made a mistake. I ought to have let Celia and Orlando go with their leashes attached to them and I automatically didn't. Even if I'd thought clearly I don't believe I could have done it, because I knew it would just have been a way of killing them. And they're such beautiful creatures. Killers themselves, but so beautiful. But it gave away that Rosalind's escape was somehow different from the others and made the police realise the whole scene had been faked.'

'And all the time you were doing this,' Fiona said wonderingly, 'you believed Annette had killed your brother.'

'Oh, my dear,' Nina said, beginning to cry again, 'if only she were worth it!'

'She did kill him, didn't she?' Arthur said, looking steadily into Jocelyn's face. 'And you've been making time for her to get away. She isn't with those schoolgirls at all. She's God knows where by now.'

Jocelyn gave a sigh of incredible weariness.

'Perhaps, Arthur. I don't know. As soon as I got back here last night after the police let the rest of us go, I took her into Swelsden, where she said she'd wait for an early train. It was still dark then, so I don't think anyone saw us drive off. Then I came home and set about getting rid of all the evidence that she was left-handed and I drove off and dumped it in that pond in the old quarry up the lane here, just before you get to the London road. As you say, I was making time for her.'

'But listen!' Susan exclaimed. 'Listen a minute! If all this is true, she couldn't possibly have killed Rob. He was killed with one of the hoes Conrad and I left by the gate, wasn't he? We took those hoes from Arthur's toolshed. And we left them by the gate when we drove into Swelsden. And I've been taking for granted Rob was killed after we did that by someone who saw the hoe when she came to the house and rang the bell and went away again without waiting for an answer. But it was before we took the hoes that we saw Jocelyn hitting Annette, and only just after we'd taken them that Orlando came swooping past us, just over our heads. I said at the time he was big enough to be Orlando . . .'

She stopped, struck dumb as she understood where her argument was taking her.

Arthur had been quicker than she. His expression had changed while she had been speaking. She saw the look of understanding appear on his face which she always found incongruous. He ought not to look so intelligent, so almost sympathetic. It was out of character.

'What a pity you thought of that, Susan,' he said. 'I'm really sorry you thought of it. But since you have . . .' The sympathy was gone. His light grey eyes were cold as stones. His hand came up with the gun in it.

Fiona gave a scream. She threw herself in front of him.

'Don't, Arthur, don't! It won't help!'

He shouted suddenly, 'Why did she have to say anything

about it? You're her sister, aren't you? Why couldn't she let us get away with it? Why should she protect that other woman?'

Fiona caught his arm. 'Don't waste time, Arthur. Let's go. We've got to go!'

From the kitchen doorway the voice of Inspector Piggott remarked quietly, 'Even that won't help very much, Mrs Laslett. Smuggling's one thing, but murder's another. You won't get very far.'

How long he had been there, how much he had heard of what Jocelyn had said, none of them knew at the time. Later they learnt that he had heard most of it. He had seen them arriving one after the other at the cottage and followed them in, but had gone round to the back door, pushing it softly open and entering just after they had returned to the sitting-room after inspecting the hole in the bathroom floor.

Massively impersonal as always, he walked forward now with a hand out as if he were expecting Arthur simply to put the gun in it.

Perhaps for an instant Arthur thought that he was going to shoot, but something about the sight of the burly man advancing straight towards him unnerved him. With all his strength he threw the gun at the inspector's face, caught Fiona by the arm, jerked the door open, taking the key as he did so, pulled Fiona out and slammed the door.

As Inspector Piggott, with a cut on one cheek where the gun had struck him, lunged at the door, they turned the key outside and went running together to the gate and their car, tumbled into it and drove off.

By the time that Conrad had run out through the kitchen, round the cottage to the front and unlocked the door, they were out of sight.

Inspector Piggott stood still in the open doorway. A thin trickle of blood was sliding down his cheek like a tear.

'They won't get far,' he said. 'They can't.'

But he was wrong. They went far, as far as anyone can go, and fast. They drove straight to the quarry into which Jocelyn had pitched what he had believed was the evidence of murder against his wife, and went over the edge of it at ninety miles an hour.

16

'We'll have to talk about it, you know, or we'll never get beyond it,' Conrad said.

It was some weeks later and he and Susan were sitting in a café together again, though this time in Fulham.

During those weeks they had not seen much of one another. Susan had stayed with Nina until after the inquests, then she had returned to London, to her bed-sitting-room, to experience a loneliness of a kind that she had never even dreamt of before. A kind of vicarious guilt, through her love for Fiona, had made her feel wholly cut off from the rest of the human race. This state of mind had terrified her, yet she had clung to her solitude with desperation as the only condition that she could bear. Every time that the telephone rang it had felt like a threat. She had spent her time working almost continually till her eyes ached and her head swam. If it had not been for occasionally seeing Conrad, whom she could endure because he knew as much about the murders as she did, she might have lost her grip on the outer world altogether, and turned into someone she was never meant to be.

The others connected with the story of murder had gone their separate ways.

Nina had put Bright's Farm and the cottage up for sale and had sold them immediately to a development company for an even larger sum than she had expected. She had kept Touchie, but had given Oliver to the Merrow children and had gone to live for the present on the island of Skyros in the Ægean, from which she had written to Susan to say that Touchie enjoyed the change of climate, that she was learning Greek, writing a book on the growth and uses of culinary herbs and, believe it or not, putting on weight.

Jocelyn and Annette had also gone abroad. Women who got themselves involved in murder, however innocently, she had been given discreetly to understand, were not what the school at which she had been a teacher required on its staff. She and Jocelyn were now roaming about in Spain with a trailer, looking for a spot where Jocelyn felt that he could settle down to write his next play.

Mrs Collis had returned to Birmingham and taken a new lodger, in whom, as seemed to be her fate, the local police were already showing signs of taking a certain interest.

There had been a few reports from the Swelsden area of a monstrous owl being seen, but they had ceased. Celia had never been heard of again. Perhaps she was still free, hunting successfully for herself, perhaps she had perished, perhaps been captured by another falconer, who had heard the tinkling of her bells and succeeded in trapping her.

The police in Swelsden, with the help of Stan Wall, had more or less pieced together the story of the smuggling and the two murders.

Stan Wall, on being arrested, had talked without restraint, had answered every question that the police had asked him, then volunteered more information still, to save himself from being suspected of complicity in the murders. Rob Riscoe had had nothing whatever to do with the smuggling, he had said. Wall didn't mind saying it, now that Arthur Laslett was dead. It was Arthur who had been his partner. Wall and Arthur had first met a year or two after the war, when Arthur had still been in the army and enjoyably engrossed in a number of small black market operations. He had not been making much money out of them, he had simply enjoyed the excitement of breaking the rules. Wall, a professional, had thought him a fool. What did you go into the game at all for, if it wasn't for the money? However, on and off, ever since then, they had kept in touch, carrying out a number of jobs together.

Arthur, perhaps because of his good education, had had a versatility that Wall admired. On the other hand, he had a recklessness which had often frightened Wall, and an explosive temper which made Wall consider him unreliable. He had always felt uneasy, working with Arthur.

A year ago they had chanced to meet after a longish interval, during which Arthur had got married. Wall had happened to be looking for a good spot for dropping smuggled goods from a plane. Arthur had said that he thought he knew of the very place. It was only about twenty miles from the coast, a cottage with a big plot of open ground behind it, and not overlooked by any house but Arthur's own. The cottage had been just about to become vacant because the old man who had lived there for the last fifty years had died and his widow was moving away to live with her married daughter in Swelsden.

Arthur had been able to tell Wall enough about the Gracies to enable him to write a plausible-sounding letter to the Riscoes claiming to be related to the old couple, which Arthur had felt sure, from what he knew of the Riscoes, would never be investigated. He had been right. Stan Wall and Sandra, as Mr and Mrs Taylor, had moved into the cottage and all had gone well with the smuggling for a good many months.

In the village Arthur and Wall had successfully concealed their relationship, Arthur never missing an opportunity to express his disapproval of his nearest neighbours and helping to spread unpleasant gossip about them in the local pub, just as he had helped to stir up antagonism to the Riscoes and tried to discredit Conrad. The more people in the place who appeared to be behaving suspiciously, the better for Arthur himself, he had thought.

A good many valuable hauls, mostly of watches and cameras, had been brought into the country during this time and profitably disposed of.

But Arthur had changed. Perhaps it had been because of that wife of his, Wall had thought, or perhaps it was just growing older, but Arthur had wanted to boss the show more and more and had wanted more and more money out of it. Wall hadn't thought that he could afford a quarrel and had let Arthur get away with a bigger percentage than had first been agreed between them, but still had found him growing steadily harder and harder to handle. When Rob Riscoe, out at twilight with his owl, had caught Wall, red-handed, picking up the parcel of watches that had just been dropped, and when Riscoe had turned out to be ready, for the sake of his own peace and quiet, to say nothing about it to the police if Wall and his girl would get out of the cottage, Wall had thought he was getting out of things pretty well and that this was obviously a good time to close down the whole operation.

But he had not said anything about this to Arthur. He had not meant to let Arthur have any of the proceeds from the last consignment. He would simply slip away with the lot and Arthur could do all his own organising after that, if he wanted to. That would teach him. It had seemed like a good time for getting rid of Sandra too, and he had left her behind to talk eagerly of going to London and to see their useless furniture off to an imaginary address there, without mentioning to her that his own destination was Dublin.

But Mrs Laslett had seen the furniture van arrive and the furniture being moved and had telephoned her husband, who had driven home from his office in the lunch-hour and had surprised Sandra just as she was about to leave the cottage. And then the one thing had happened to which Stan Wall had given no thought, of which he had had no fear. Not a violent man himself, he had never dreamt that Arthur could turn violent. Though Wall had known of Arthur's capacity for rage, he had never seen it completely out of hand. In the police-station he swore and wept and pleaded with the police to believe him that he had never guessed that when Arthur realised how he had been tricked, he would take Sandra by the throat and crush the life out of her.

That was Stan Wall's story.

What remained had been supplied by Inspector Piggott and much of it, inevitably, was guesswork. He believed that when Arthur had found Sandra dead on his hands, he had decided to dispose of her body after dark, had left her in the cottage, locking the door behind him, and had not returned until night, when, by the light of the moon, he had suddenly found himself, incredibly, face to face with a ten foot python.

186

When it had entered the cottage there was no way of knowing. Perhaps it had come in during the morning, when the furniture was being taken out by the front door and no one was paying much attention to what was happening at the back.

Whatever the truth of that might be, Arthur had been terrified, but so had the python and it had made straight for what it took to be a bolt-hole in the bathroom floor, but in fact was a brick cavity with no outlet of any kind. Arthur had had the presence of mind to clap the boards back in place and screw them down, then he had dragged Sandra's body away into the woods, hiding it among the brambles.

Perhaps he would have taken more trouble about how he hid it, if he had not half-wanted it to be found. For he must have been thinking at that time that Stan Wall would be suspected of the murder. But in fact Arthur had already made his first irretrievable blunder. Wall, with his withered arm, could never have killed Sandra in the way that Arthur had killed her.

Having realised this, he was more careful next time. This time there would be no mistake. The evidence would point straight at Wall. The murderer would be left-handed.

Arthur's decision to kill Rob must have been quickly made when Rob gave away, just before the Merrow children threw the brick through the window, that he knew of Wall's smuggling activities and had used this knowledge to make Wall move from the cottage. For how much more did Rob know? A reserved creature, going his own way, living his life according to his own strange rules, when would he spring some trap on Arthur and destroy him? It would be best to be rid of him.

That evening Arthur had waited until Mrs Collis had left the house, then he had said that he was going to bed and was not to be disturbed at any cost, then he had gone straight out to the garden shed, taken a heavy hoe, gone through the woods to the studio, where he had known that he would find Rob, waking the falcon, and being a strong and moderately ambidextrous man, had not found it difficult to hold the hoe in his left hand and strike Rob from behind. It had gone off quickly and smoothly. Probably Rob had not even been able to turn, with the excited bird bating off on his fist, to see who his murderer was.

But then there had been nothing but misfortune for Arthur. Wall's alibi had been impregnable and Jocelyn had come along and carefully got rid of all the evidence that pointed to a left-handed murderer. But, worse still, Susan and Conrad had gone to the tool-shed and taken out the very hoe with which Arthur had killed Rob before he had cleaned it properly, and they had left it where it was certain to attract the attention of the police. Fiona's invention of a visitor who had come to the door and rung the bell after Susan had gone out had been an attempt to cover this.

In the Fulham café, sitting over hamburgers and chips, Susan and Conrad had not had much to say to one another. Conrad was starting his new job next day. He should have been full of it. Nervous, perhaps, but excited. Instead, Susan had found him unusually subdued. For the last few weeks he had been living with his mother and stepfather in their flat in Westminster, but he had now found a small flat for himself not far from Susan's bed-sitting-room. They had been to the theatre together and afterwards he had not seemed to want to talk about the new job, or himself, or any of the things about which he was generally all too loquacious, and neither of them had wanted to talk of Swelsden or the murders. So, for a time they had worked hard at pulling the play to pieces, then they had fallen silent.

It was after the silence had grown long that he had at last given a sigh and in the tone of someone forcing himself unwillingly to face the inevitable, had said that they would have to talk about what had happened to them or they would never get beyond it.

He went on, 'They did do it on purpose, didn't they, Susan? I mean, with the death penalty gone, they wouldn't have been hanged. So they must have wanted to end like that.'

'Of course,' Susan said.

There was another silence.

Susan broke it this time. 'People don't change. I ought to have realised that. I ought to have known Fiona couldn't really have settled down into the calm, satisfied housewife she seemed to have turned into. When I think of it now, it seems fantastic that I ever believed it. She was always wild for excitement when she was a girl, and she didn't change. I think that's why she was so much in love with Arthur. He gave her the excitement she craved for. That's why they kept on with the smuggling, I'm sure. Just for the excitement. They can't have needed the money.'

'Well, I don't know, everyone seems to need money, however much they've got,' Conrad said. 'I'm awfully scared myself of starting to need money. How does one know where it's going to end?'

'Yes, I know what you mean,' Susan said. 'And of course they were living right above Arthur's income – his salary as an accountant, I mean. I suppose I ought to have realised that too – only I don't know much about how far money goes, once one gets out of the studentship class. I suppose I sort of imagined Arthur was clever with investments and that sort of thing.'

'He got quite a handsome profit out of the smuggling, according to Stan Wall,' Conrad reminded her.

'Oh yes, they liked money and I suppose actually they were getting to like it more and more, but I still think it was the excitement that meant most to them, particularly to Fiona. I don't think she ever thought of smuggling seriously as a crime, or dreamt for a moment it could lead to murder. And when it did, you know, when it dawned on her that Arthur must have killed Sandra, she began by going to pieces. I remember that day in the garden, when you came with the news that they'd found Sandra's body, Fiona couldn't face it. She started to cry and almost lost her head. She was always rather like that in any crisis, yet I couldn't really understand it. But she was terribly in love with Arthur, so she pulled herself together and stuck to him. Conrad . . .'

'Yes?'

'I was only thinking . . .' She went on thinking for a while before she went on. 'Look at what being in love with Arthur did to Fiona.'

'To be fair to him,' Conrad said, 'perhaps it was the other way round.'

'All right, but look at what being in love with Annette did to Jocelyn. He suspected her of horrible things she hadn't done and at the same time developed a morbid sort of mania to protect her.'

'That's what's sometimes called true love, isn't it?' Conrad said.

'Well then, take Nina and Rob – I suppose they cared for each other quite a lot, and yet I don't believe Nina's really unhappy now. She's grieving in a way, and yet she also acts like someone who's been released from a tremendous strain.'

'And all this makes you think that love's a bad idea,' Conrad said. 'It distorts the judgment and rots the moral fibre.'

'All I mean is, I don't much like what I've been seeing of it.'

'You haven't touched on my kind of love,' he said. 'Clear-sighted, hard-headed, and kicking back when I get kicked too hard in the teeth. You might think about it.'

'Oh, Conrad!' She shook her head at him sadly. 'You aren't clear-sighted or hard-headed and you don't kick back. You're only saying that to see what it sounds like, aren't you? You always say you have to say a thing or write a thing before you know if you mean it.'

'Well, how does it sound?' he asked, smiling at her across the congealing hamburgers.